I0738213

THE BLUE BICYCLE

by

Bob Mustin

GRIDLEY FIRES

First Published by *Gridley Fires Books*, 6/15/2017

Gridley Fires Books and its logo are trademarked
by
Gridley Fires Books Publishing

Artie — 1980

Yeaah, the bell! No more school stuff, least 'til Monday. My sneaks squeak, I'm walking so fast. You can hear it, even with everybody laughing and goofing around. Daddy's coming to see me in a coupla minutes. Nobody's watching, so I'm gonna run and get my bike. I can't wait!

"Artie!"

Uh oh. Mrs. Winslow. Now I gotta stop, see what she wants. She's the principal, but two years ago she was my first grade teacher. That was when Mama cried all the time, just 'fore Daddy moved out.

"Are you riding or walking today, Artie?"

She looks me over.

"I rode my bike."

"What's that on your face?"

I don't say 'cause I don't want her to know Brent gave me some chocolate, and I ate it in class.

"Wait right here," she tells me. She goes to her office. She's got a round mirror, the same size as my face.

She smiles when she stoops and says, "Tell me what's wrong with this picture, young man."

Well, first off, my hair is all messed up. Mama calls me a sandy-haired mop-top, but I can't make it stay in place, no matter what. So now I comb it a little with my fingers and push it down in the back where it stands up. My cheeks are a little bit red, but that wouldn't show if I didn't have this white skin, almost like Daddy's. My nose is dripping, but I think it's 'cause it's too thin to store up much snot. I sniff, real hard. Then I laugh.

I never noticed my ears sticking out like that. And the chocolate gunk around my mouth makes me look weird, like the clown I saw at the circus with Papa Merle last year—the one who snuck up and scared me. I start licking at the chocolate. Mrs. Winslow pushes my hand away, fishes in her pocket for a Kleenex, and wipes off what's left.

She's looking at something outside, so I twist around to see. Huh. Nothing but the same old Weaverville houses. And a bunch of tree branches swooshing around like they're dancing. The sky's real blue with a little cloud scooting along. Mama says that's the way it always is here in the mountains in April. 'Cept when it rains.

Mrs. Winslow kind of sits on her heels and makes a line with her mouth, the way Mama does when she's looking at me real hard. After that, she pulls my jeans up and buttons my coat all the way. I start squirming 'cause I gotta go. I can't keep my daddy waiting.

"All right, Artie," she says. "But no more running."

I'm out the door in a blue streak. That's one of Mama's sayings, and it's true, I run pretty fast. There's my bike, the cool one with the high handlebars. Mama says it was a StingRay Krate when she got it, before Papa Merle painted it blue. You can still see where the name used to be.

Now I can't get the key to go in the lock, and I think a bad word I got from Daddy. I don't say it, though, and finally the lock comes off. So I jump on and push hard on the wood blocks Papa Merle fixed on the pedals. It's hard to get started. I almost fall down, I'm wobbling so much. A lady in a van sees me and waves for me to go first. The stickshift won't work, so I push really hard on the pedals. Uhff, it still won't go. The lady smiles and waves at me and goes on by.

Boy, it's Friday, and Daddy's coming! He said he'd take me to the park at Lake Louise. We're gonna play catch. He played in Little League when he was little like me, but he got in some trouble. After that, he quit.

I hit the stickshift real hard, and this time the chain goes clackety-clack. The bike jerks, and all of a sudden it's easy to pedal. The wind's whistling down South Main Street. It makes my eyes water. Now it's in my ears, telling me, wheee, hurry up, Artie!

I pedal really hard. Pretty soon, I'm almost at the top, where you can see between the houses to the Balcrank plant. The mountains look like a big pile of dirty clothes, except they're purple.

Uh oh. I didn't pick up my stuff this morning. Gotta do that 'fore Daddy comes. It's gonna be cold over at Lake

Louise when we play catch. That's all right, though. I'll wear some mittens with my ball glove.

Daddy used to be in the carnival before he married Mama. That was after the bad thing happened in his head and he quit school. In the carnival he threw knives. Mama—her name's Marie—she used to say she was glad she didn't know him then. He'd hear that and say all the other carnies loved him, and she woulda too. Then he'd laugh real loud and hug her.

A coupla weeks ago, I wanted him to teach me to throw knives like that. So the next day he showed up making funny faces, and I think he was drinking some. He borrowed my bicycle pump to blow up this big doll that looked like a lady with a little place between her legs.

I pointed to it. "What's that for, Daddy?"

He laughed real soft. "Walk up to it an say hello," he said. "Say it real loud."

It was dumb, but I did it.

"Now," he said, "put your ear up to it and tell me what you hear."

I didn't hear nothing. I told him so.

"Nothing?"

"Nossir."

"You don't hear no voice coming back? Telling you what to do?" Then he slapped one of his skinny legs and laughed so hard he doubled over.

That was dumb, too.

Then he stopped laughing and told me, "All right, boy, stand it up next to that big oak." While I did that, he went back to his truck and pulled out this big box and set it on the ground. It had all these big, shiny knives inside. He picked out four he said were his favorites. He spread 'em around in one hand, and pulled one out by the shiny blade part. Then he winked and said, "Watch this."

It went whistling through the air. "Phwhht." It stuck in the tree, right beside the lady doll's head. That was so cool! He did it three more times, and every time the points went thunnng! when they stuck in the tree. It was only a play-lady, but you could tell if it was a real one she wouldn't be worried.

"Let me, Daddy, let me!" I hollered.

Right then, Mama came to the door and walked across the yard to see what I was doing. She started frowning when she saw the doll.

"Casey," she yelled, "are you out of your mind? What if some of the neighbors see that thing?" She was shaking her finger real hard, and that always means she's really, really mad. "Artie," she said, "get away from it."

"Daddy wanted me to say hello to it, Mama, right there." I pointed at the little pocket.

Daddy was laughing to himself with his head down and kinda pawing the ground with one foot.

"Casey Royal!"

I thought she was going to make her throat sore, she screamed so hard. Then she pulled out one of the knives and stabbed the doll.

Daddy laughed some more. He made his arms and legs move like the doll did when the air went out. So Mama pulled another knife out and flung it real hard, and it stuck in the ground by his foot. That made him laugh even harder, so she stomped back in the house and slammed the door.

Daddy quit laughing then, but it took a minute. He worked his mouth back and forth. Then he spit some brown gunk. Snuff, I think. "She don't look like her old self. She been sick again?"

"Yessir," I told him. "She's got the cramps. She spends a lotta time in bed."

"Huh. Well, she looks like she's lost some weight too."

He's so skinny himself, and white looking—you can see blue stuff under his skin. And he's tall, not like Mama. She's short and has dark skin. She's pretty, too. But she frowns a lot when he comes around now. She told me he's got lots of problems, and one is he's always been a lady's man. She said they like him, even with that long face and big eyes that look like they're too close together. I guess liking ladies back is okay, though. Mama's a lady, the best one I know.

She says the other big problem is he gets too quiet sometimes. He won't laugh, for days and days. And he won't talk, no matter what. He mashes his lips together so hard you can't tell he's got a mouth. When he does that, he looks like he's maybe gonna cry. Sometimes when you say something to him about it, his face gets red. His Adam's apple goes up and down. But sometimes you can't get him to be quiet. He yells and uses bad words and kicks stuff. When it gets real bad, he scares me and Mama. But he hasn't done that in a long time.

Now my pedals feel mushy. Then they run away from me, they're going so fast. So I lift up my feet and lean over, 'tween the handlebars, to pick up speed. Going fast makes me laugh. That squawking jaybird thinks I'm like him. Well, I am. I'm flying!

A lady in a big green car just honked for me to get out of the way. She frowned at me, and then she whizzed on by. But I don't care. I'm going as fast as I can, and I'm almost home.

This time I don't drop my bike in the carport like I do sometimes when I'm in a hurry. If Mama sees it in the drive, she'll point at it and frown 'til I stand it up and chain it to a post.

Daddy's truck's not here. He's late most of the time, though. Mama says he'll be late for his own funeral.

She left me a grape juice in the refrigerator. I punch the straw in and take a big sip and start looking for her. The TV's on, one Daddy got somewhere before he moved out. Mama says it cost a lot. She's not there. Not taking a nap.

Hey, all right! She picked up my clothes and some other junk I left laying around.

But all of a sudden the house feels big, and it's cold. Where'd she go? My heart's beating like crazy, and my breathing's real loud. So I open the back door and peek out. Something makes a clank, off to one side.

"Artie? I'm in the garden, Artie. Come on out here, and please close the door."

Now my hands are all tingly. The tingles run up my arms, and that makes me laugh. Mama's here! She's out back, where Papa Merle built some timbers to hold up dirt for the garden. She's sitting there, mounding up dirt around the little plants so they won't freeze. A plastic cover's all spread out, the way we talked about this morning. 'Fore it gets dark, I'm gonna help her pull it over the garden. We'll hold it down with a bunch of rocks.

I slip on the grass, put a big stain on my knee. But I don't worry about it, 'cause I gotta find out about Daddy.

"Mama, did he call? Is he still coming?"

She turns around and smiles, like she always does when I come home. Her hair's long and brown. The wind fluffs it out, and it keeps getting in her eyes. She brushes some of it back over her ears. Then she reaches over and squeezes my arm, kinda hard. She smells wet. She got all sweaty working in the garden, I guess. The blue shirt she has on is real soft. Her breath feels nice. It's warm.

Uh oh. Now she's gonna cry.

I reach up and wipe the tears off. That makes her cry even more. I can't wipe all of it.

"No, honey." She kinda chokes like this when she says something she doesn't want to. "Casey won't be coming to see you."

Something's wrong. I know something's wrong. Feels like a big rock is sitting on my chest. I wanna yell, but I can't get it out. Can't say anything. I must be making noise, though, 'cause she keeps saying, "Shhh, honey, shhh." Then she takes the grape juice and tips it up for me.

After a minute, I can talk a little. "Not at all, Mama? Is he coming later? It'll be dark soon. We can't play catch then." I still feel like yelling, 'cause it's gotta be the fits he has, the thing he's got wrong in his head. I don't want him to be sick again.

She picks me up, but she grunts 'cause I'm pretty big now. Then she sets me on her lap. She's rubbing her eyes with both hands, and I do that to mine, too. She's making me cry. I wanna get even closer, so I lean on her chest. She's real soft there.

"Can he come tomorrow, Mama? Can we play catch tomorrow?"

I bet he won't come, though. I know how Daddy is when he's sick.

She gives me a sad look, but behind it you can tell she's mad. "Artie, listen to me. Casey won't be coming to see you today, and he won't be coming tomorrow. Not ever."

"He's not?" That makes me feel kinda weird. No! I got a dark spot on my jeans. I promised I wouldn't do that again. I'm eight now, but I can't help it. No! The spot's getting bigger, and you can feel it, like sticking your finger under the kitchen faucet.

She picks me up off her lap, makes me stand where she can see my jeans. I start kicking, 'cause I don't want her to see the spot. Now it's down my leg and my shoe's getting sopped. My foot's cold. Daddy's not coming. Not ever, she said. What's that mean?

"Artie," she says. She squeezes me against her again.

"I'm sorry, Mama, I'm sorry. I didn't mean to." I keep on crying.

"I know, Artie. Go change, please?"

Now I don't care anymore. I just want to hold on to her the way a little baby does. I'm a little baby, peeing in my pants. It's my fault. The peeing, I mean. Daddy's not coming. Did I do something wrong? Mama told me once he didn't act all that bad before I came.

Finally I stop crying and say, "He won't ever come again?" I want to know, just in case.

"I'm so sorry, Artie. He had an opportunity, he said. It's in California, and he's moving there. He stopped by an hour or so ago, and he gave me a little money."

"But why didn't he come by school? Couldn't he leave tomorrow?"

"You know how he is, honey, he doesn't like confrontations."

Conder. Frin. Kayshon. That's what she always called it when she had to tell me or Daddy something we wouldn't like. He didn't want to see me, that's why he didn't come to school. He left me and Mama, and now he's going away, over to California. I start crying, real hard this time. My shoe squishes from the pee.

She stands, starts humming and swings me around. She always says it's dancing when we do that. It makes everything better, she says. Sometimes it does, but this time I can't stop crying. I need to crawl up close. That's the only thing that'll make it better.

"It's going to be okay, honey," she says. "We'll manage somehow. It's okay its okay its okay. Humm hummn humm." Then she puts me down. "Now go change."

A car drives up. A police car. A man gets out. "Mrs. Royal?" he says.

Mama lets go and pats me on the butt. I run for the door, so the man won't see what I did. But I can watch from behind the screen door.

He smiles at Mama. Then he ah-hums to get something clear in his throat. "Is Casey James Royal your husband?"

"He was. We were divorced six months ago." She wipes at her eyes. Then she brushes hair off her face. "What's wrong, officer?"

"Ma'am, your ex robbed a couple of students at the college in Mars Hill just after noon today."

Mama's mouth falls open and her eyes get real big. "Casey? Are you sure?"

"They got the tag number off his pickup. This was the address given."

"Oh, no. He didn't hurt anyone, did he? I know Casey has his problems, but he'd never—"

"No, ma'am, no one was hurt. But he took a sizeable sum from them. In the neighborhood of four hundred dollars."

Mama makes a noise, kind of soft-like. She pushes a hand in her pocket and pulls out some money, all rolled up. I can barely hear it when she says, "He gave me this money, not an hour ago."

The policeman takes it and counts it. "That's about the right amount."

Her head's down. I think she's gonna yell for sure, 'cause I know she's mad at Daddy now. "Go ahead," she says. "Take it."

"I'm sorry about this, ma'am. I'll give you a receipt, but I expect the judge'll give the money back to the college kids." He puts a hand on her shoulder. I want him to hug her the way Daddy used to when he was sorry he made her cry.

"I hate to ask you this," he says, "but he isn't here, is he?"

She jerks her head up and makes a little wrinkled circle with her mouth. I know she's really mad now. "No," she says. She rubs one foot on the drive, real hard.

"I'm going to have to look around a bit. Mind if I go inside?"

"Go on," she says. "I know it's your job."

He looks at me, inside the screen door. I forgot about my pants. So I run to my room and find a clean pair and some unders. I go to the bathroom and shut the door.

A coupla minutes later, he knocks. "You in there, son?"

"Yessir."

My clean jeans were wadded up in the drawer, and I can't get them on.

"You can take care of your business in a minute, young fella, but right now I need to look around."

I have to sit on the toilet to get my jeans straightened out. Now they're on, but I need some socks. And I forgot my other shoes.

The door opens and he peeks in. He takes off his hat and smiles before he comes inside. "It's okay," he says. "I don't bite." He shoos me back to the door so he can look behind the shower curtain.

Then he waves me back some more, and I go in the hall. He smiles again while he's walking by. Then he pushes hard on the door to Mama's room and hurries in. By the time I get my socks and shoes on, he's finished looking around. He goes outside and starts talking to Mama. She slumps a little. He says something and puts his arm around her.

She takes a little card he hands her and puts her shoulders back, like she's trying to stand up tall. I see her do that around men sometimes. I think she likes him. He gets in and drives off.

Daddy really did that stuff? I crawl up on the couch and start watching TV. She comes in and sits beside me. She takes the remote away and pushes MUTE. She's going to tell me something. It's going to be a conder. Frind. She's going to tell me something bad.

"Artie," she says, "do you understand what's happened?"

"Yes'm." I do, kinda, but I don't wanna talk about it. The cartoons are on. They're funny. I wanna watch TV, but I can't, 'cause she's gonna tell me something bad.

All of a sudden, Daddy's voice is talking in my head. I can see his face. We're at Lake Louise, and he's rolling the ball, the way he did one day last year, the first day we played catch. I was afraid of the ball when he started throwing it, but he kept telling me it's okay, in baseball you gotta catch the ball if you want to throw it. "And throwing it's kinda like the knives," he said. "You have to let go of it, so it can act the way it's s'posed to." I said okay, and I caught on pretty fast after that. Now when it's in the air it don't scare me. We went for ice cream, and he told me he thought I'd be a big league baseball player. He said he was gonna work with me on it. I'd have to work real hard, though.

"You gonna do that?" he said.

"Yessir."

"Even if it gets in the way of school?"

"Uh huh."

"All right," he said. "That school stuff's for the birds, boy. They don't teach you anything. Out here in the world, that's where you learn. Out here, you can do things nobody's ever done before."

Now Mama clicks off the TV. "You understand Casey did something wrong?"

"He took some money."

"You understand that's wrong, don't you?"

I don't, but I nod like I do. He gave the money to us.

"I'm going to have to get a full-time job," she says. "When I do, I won't be here when you come home from school. You're going to have to help out around the house."

"Yes'm."

"You going to be all right by yourself?"

I want to tell her I will, but I don't know for sure.

"I'll get Mrs. Epperson next door to check on you."

That'll be cool. She makes cookies. But I'll be by myself after she brings the cookies. Now I'm feeling sorta weird, like I did when Daddy left.

She hugs me, then starts giggling. She runs a finger under my arm and tickles me.

"Stop it!" I don't want to play, but now I'm giggling, too, and that makes her laugh.

"That's my big boy," she says.

Mama got a job at a restaurant, out on Merrimon. Most of the time she's happy. She takes in the money, and sometimes she stays late to count it. It wears her out, she says, but she sleeps all night. She says she hasn't done that in a long time.

It's not so bad, her not being here, 'cause I have a buncha stuff to do, and then some homework. She hates coming back to a messy place. It puts her in a bad mood. So she showed me how to wash clothes. I can do the dishes if I stand on a chair. Once a week I run the vacuum. The best part is she always brings something home from the restaurant for supper. I get so hungry. But now we can eat the minute she comes in. Most times, there's a little left over for lunch the next day. Sometimes she even brings dessert.

Today I did everything perfect. It's her birthday. I cleaned up her room and made the bed. Mrs. Epperson started the lawn mower so I could cut the yard. We had cookies and Cokes after that, and she brought over a cake a little bit ago. It's on the dining room table, right in the middle. We had some candles left over from my birthday, so I put 'em on. I didn't have enough, but Mama won't mind. And I made some punch with grape juice and ginger ale. Papa Merle's coming over, too. It's gonna be a surprise party!

A car drives up, and before I can look out, a door slams. She's here. The lady she rides with drives off.

Mama calls out, "Artie! Come put your bike away, please."

Oh, man. Hope she doesn't find out I rode all the way to Lake Louise after I mowed the yard and had the cookies and Coke. The stickshift worked great this time. When I'm on the bike and really ride fast, it's like nothing can bother me. I don't have to think about Casey—I call him that now, 'cause he's not my daddy anymore. Sometimes I don't think about Mama working. And I don't even think about being by myself after school. I wish I could feel like that all the time.

Mama won't like Papa Merle seeing the bike where it might get run over. Her daddy gave it to her before he was killed in that war. After he died, she moved in with Papa Merle, and he painted it blue.

She's holding a paper bag with a big greasy spot on the side. She's not smiling. That's bad. Oh, man. I get the bike chained to the post right before Papa Merle drives up.

He's real big. He's so fat he has to huff and puff to get out of the car. He has sorta dark skin and looks a lot like Mama, 'cause they're part Indian, he says. His voice goes boom in the carport. He runs a hand through that black hair of his that Mama says is stiff as bristles. He takes the bag and hands it to me. Then he picks her up and swings her around. They're both laughing now, so he puts her down and gets his fiddle out of the car, and we go inside.

"Hey, hey," he says, and he gives Mama another big hug. "You're looking pretty good for twenty-four, little girl."

"Twenty-five, Grandpa. And you look pretty round for seventy-seven. You quit your diet again, didn't you?" Now she's talking like him, like the words are coming from deep down inside and out her nose.

"Ah, honey, at my age I ain't got time for doing the right thing, just the happy thing."

"Grandpa," she says.

"There's the cake," I say, "and some punch I made. Come on."

"We need to eat supper first," Mama says. "I'm not going to let you two fill up on sweets."

"It's your birthday," Papa Merle tells her. "Back in Acadia we always did everything backwards on birthdays."

She pokes him in his round stomach. Mama just comes up to his shoulder.

He laughs. "Cut the cake, little girl. Then I'll play some, and you can dance a little bit."

Now I'm jumping around like a grasshopper. It's going to be a real party with Papa Merle here. He went through a war a long time ago. He fought some Germans, but he says he never forgot how to have a good time. I'm yelling when I say, "Mrs. Epperson made it. It's chocolate, with cream cheese icing." It looks so good I have to wipe some slobber on my shirtsleeve.

"I'm gonna light the candles," says Papa Merle, "and you make a wish, Miss Twenty-five."

We sing happy birthday to her. She joins in and points at herself when she sings "to me." Then she blows. They don't all go out. One's a trick candle I put on. We all laugh and clap, and she blows on it some more, but the flame keeps coming back. Papa Merle finally puts it out, and she gets out a knife.

"Make it a big one, hon," says Papa Merle.

She marks off a skinny piece. He laughs and moves the knife, pushes on her hand and flips a big fat chunk on a paper plate.

He takes a bite and says, "Mm, mm, that'll make you hit your daddy." He stops grinning and peeks at me, then gives Mama a look. But it's just a saying he likes, and I don't mind, 'cause it don't have anything to do with Casey. Mama and me, we're doing okay by ourselves, better than with him. I don't miss him much at all now.

The phone rings.

No! It's Casey, from California. He wants to talk to Mama. She takes the phone and goes to the bedroom. A coupla minutes go by. She starts yelling. Me and Papa Merle can hear what she's saying. Papa Merle makes a fist and bangs it on the table. I kinda know what he's thinking, but he doesn't say it.

"What'd he want, hon?" he says when she comes back. He's frowning, real hard.

"What he always wants, money." That's all she says. Then she wipes her nose and pours punch in some paper cups. We finish, and Papa Merle smiles and grabs our hands. He takes us to the living room.

"What we need is a little music. Make some space for dancing, okay?" He pops open his case, picks up his bow, and rosins up. Me and Mama move the coffee table and a coupla chairs over to the wall. The rug's a big green one. It's sitting in the middle of the room, but the wood floor shows around the edges. It's big enough to dance on, though.

When Papa Merle finishes tuning up his fiddle, he draws his bow across the strings, and you can see the rosin scoot across them. He leans over his fiddle and starts playing. The music sounds like a bug jumping.

He tunes one more time. "We going to do some Chéticamp music. You teach the boy to two-step?"

Mama squints at me. She says, "Yes, I've been teaching Artie some. I think I remembered it right."

"Now, I know you can't forget that," he says to her. He sets his fiddle on a chair. He grabs Mama, and off they go, from one end of the rug to the other. "Go ahead and do a little bit of it, too, son," he says when they stop.

Mama pulls me off the couch. We start the tick-a-tack-a-toe thing she taught me, and Papa Merle plunks it on his fiddle's little string.

"That's the ting-a-ling part," he says.

Mama nods, and then she turns to me. "Remember on the music tape, the triangle part?"

She dances some more, and I do it, too. I have to be careful, though. Her feet are moving really fast and I don't wanna get in the way.

Papa Merle sits on the couch. He taps a foot and starts playing. Mama grabs my hands, and off we go. He starts playing faster, faster. It's kinda like riding my bike down the hill to school. It feels like I'm flying. I'm not thinking about it now, not thinking about anything, just dancing. Mama says your feet can think for themselves, and that's so. It's sorta like we're in the air over the rug, sorta like the rosin scooting over Papa Merle's strings.

Mama falls on the couch. I'm glad, 'cause my feet finally forgot how the steps go. She's panting and sweating a little, and her face is splotchy red. Then my feet start tapping again, by themselves.

Papa Merle laughs and points his bow. "That's good, son, they learning. Next time they won't forget a thing."

"That was fun, Grandpa," says Mama. "Thanks."

He nods. "Almost makes me forget I left Acadia."

Mama has a sad face now. She looks down. "Sometimes I wish we were all there," she says. "Sometimes I wish you'd never left."

"It's like I always told you, hon, I had to do my duty, just like your papa did."

Now her mouth is scrunched up. I think she's gonna break out crying. She says, "No, you didn't have any duty, Grandpa. Canada turned you down because of your flat feet. But you just had to get into it, didn't you? You just had to come to the States, where they'd take you."

Papa Merle laughs a little. "Don't forget, little girl, I met your grandmamma down here after the war. You wouldn't be around at all if I hadn't done that. Besides, the mountains, they like the ones back home. Sometimes in the winter it's almost like being there."

"I know the story, Grandpa. They called out to you."

"That's right. You don't believe it, but they did. I could hear 'em. But I promise you this. I'm gonna move back 'fore I die. I'm gonna take you. No doubt about it, Nova Scotia's in your blood. I can see it when you dance."

That makes her feel better, I think. She smiles. "You still pine for the sea, Grandpa? You still want to be out in the fishing boats?"

He looks at his shoes. "Always did, hon, always will. Just didn't happen again, that's all."

Nobody says a thing for a minute, then Mama smiles. "Anybody hungry?"

"Me!" I yell. She frowns. I've been yelling too much, and that's not good manners.

"You know me," says Papa Merle, "I could always eat."

She tears open the bag. The food's cold, so she puts the vegetables in pots. Then the grilled chicken goes in the oven, and pretty soon we're eating. When it's all gone, Papa Merle talks Mama into another piece of cake. I hold out my plate, too.

It's way past my bedtime when he packs up his fiddle and hugs her. Then he nods over at me. "What you gonna tell him, Marie? A custody suit ain't nothing to sneeze at."

"Shh, Grandpa." Mama mouths something at him I can't see.

"He ought to know something. What if Casey tries to pick him up sometime when you ain't here? I'm afraid to think what he's capable of."

Mama kisses him, says, "I'll take care of it."

"You promise, now."

"Promise."

Before I can ask what a suit is, Mama chases Papa Merle out the door. She locks it and shoos me into the bathroom to brush and put on my peejays. She comes in my room to kiss me goodnight. I'm thinking about what Papa Merle said. I'm thinking about it so much I ask her about it.

"It's nothing much," she says. "I got a letter from a lawyer, somebody Casey hired before he went to California."

Things've been good since he left. Mama's happy, even though she's working at that restaurant and stays tired a lot. But I can tell Casey's calls get her upset.

"Casey wrote you?" I said.

"Not exactly. A lawyer wrote for him. But don't you worry, okay? I had a talk with a lawyer, too, and he says Casey won't be allowed to cause us any trouble."

"I thought he forgot about us, Mama. Why's he want to cause trouble?" But now I'm wondering what it'd be like if he did come around. Maybe we could play catch or something.

"Shh," she says. "Go to sleep." She starts rubbing circles on the sides of my head, the way she does when I have those dreams. Sometimes I have dreams, like I'm awake and sleeping at the same time. After that, I can't go back to sleep unless she rubs those circles. Now she kisses me. I don't remember anything else after that.

Papa Merle took the blocks off my bike pedals last Saturday. Then we fixed the stickshift and the brakes. Mama told him not to do all that, 'cause it was almost Halloween, and it'd be too cold for me to ride much. But he did it anyway. So Mama bought me a new back tire. My legs are longer now, and I can go real, real fast. That means I can get out in traffic without any trouble. It feels like I'm getting away with something when I go so fast. Mama says that's Casey coming out in me.

But she finally told me I could ride some today. She isn't going to let me go trick or treating, though. There's too much devilment going on, she says. So I've been riding up and down the hill. Now I back off and hit the brakes. The back wheel grabs real nice. A car honks and passes real close, right before I get to the drive. My front wheel makes a fart and slides out from under. I fall and bang up my elbow. Oh. My knee's bleeding, too.

It don't hurt much, but the skin's off my elbow. There's a big hole in my jeans. Blood's making the threads stick to my knee. Oh, man. The front wheel's bent. I think the frame is, too.

I call Papa Merle. My voice keeps on shaking, but I'm trying not to make a big deal out of it. "I skidded, Papa Merle. The front wheel's bent. Maybe the frame, too."

"The frame, huh? That's bad." He grunts. I know he's trying to picture it. "Just stand it up, okay? I'm coming over tomorrow. We'll have us a look. Get the blood cleaned up, now, you hear? Your mama don't need to be fretting about that with all she's got going on."

I get the dishes done and put a load of unders and socks and towels in the dryer. Then a car drives up. Somebody's letting Mama off early. But it's not the lady she rides to work with. It's the owner lady from the restaurant. Mama looks worried.

"Call Grandpa," she says. She locks the door. Her cough is worse now, and that's probably Casey's fault. He calls her every day. They fight, and she always yells at him.

"But I just talked to him, Mama."

"Artie, call him, please."

Then I notice it. She has a spot around one of her eyes and her lip's puffy. It's Casey, I know it's Casey. He did that!

He showed up all messy and drunk a coupla days ago in a beat-up old car. He yelled through the door that he drove straight through from California to see us. Then he started banging and yelling some more. He was going to break the door down, he said. Mama held the phone to the window. She told him she called the cops. That scared him, and he drove off. After a little while, he called. He and Mama had another big fight. She started crying, so I took the phone and told him to go away. He got real quiet for a minute, then he started laughing. But it wasn't the way he used to laugh. It sounded mean.

"Tell your mama I'm gonna see her," he said. "And I'm gonna take you off with me. We're gonna have us some fun."

"You stay away, Casey," I yelled. Mama was all curled up on the rug and moaning. It was those cramps again. "You leave us alone!"

"You calling me by my name now? You little shit, you don't have no respect at all. I got a good mind not to make you a baseball player like I was going to."

"You go to hell."

"Cussing me now, too, huh?" He started that laugh again. "You tell your mama," he said. "You tell her."

Mama got up. We hugged, and she ran herself a drink of water. That was when the police drove up.

"You all right in there?" the policeman yelled. "Hello?"

Mama unlocked and let him in.

"One of your neighbors called," he said. "She reported yelling."

Mama talked first, then me. We told him all about it.

"Is he dangerous?" the man asked Mama. "I mean, is he violent?"

Mama scrunched her shoulders. "I don't—"

"Yeah," I said. "He's crazy. He scared Mama."

The policeman got Mama to tell him what Casey's car looked like. That was the last we heard until today.

So now I call Papa Merle back.

"Casey's a damn skunk," Papa Merle says, "an honest to goodness polecat. Okay, I'll be right over. Tell your Mama to lock the doors and windows and turn on the outside light. And you might tell the neighbors to be on the lookout."

She locks everything up. I call Mrs. Epperson. She tells me everyone's there for us. Her husband'll keep the trick and treaters away so they don't get hurt. Right after I hang up, the old car pulls up to the curb and Casey gets out. He has a baseball bat, starts staggering around and yelling. Mama runs to the bedroom and shuts the door. What am I gonna do if he breaks in? But he just stays out there, yelling and waving the bat. Huh. I don't think he wants to break in. He looks scared.

I think about that for a while. I'm not afraid of him. I think about it some more. He's been drinking. It's just his big mouth, that's all. I think about going outside and yelling back, but I don't.

Papa Merle drives up. He parks behind Casey and gets out. They say a few things. Casey swings the bat, but he misses. Papa Merle jerks it out of his hands, and he hits Casey on the butt with it. Casey comes up swinging. Papa Merle hits him again, this time hard, on his knees. He hits him again, on the back. He hits him some more.

All of a sudden, police cars come from all 'round. A man jumps out of one and grabs Papa Merle. It takes two of them to hold him. Casey starts mouthing off. They throw him in the back of a police car. They put Papa Merle in another one.

The phone rings. Mama takes it to her room. It's Mrs. Epperson again, I think. Then neighbors come out of houses like ants off a hill. It's all over.

It's after nine when we get Papa Merle out of jail and take him to our place. He's still mad. He stomps around the living room and yells the way Casey used to.

"They got nothing they can hold him for," he says. "He'll be out of the hospital in a couple of days. They'll accuse him in court, but then what you think'll happen? He'll come right back over here after the boy."

"Grandpa, go on home, please," Mama says. "I need to talk to Artie."

"You right, baby girl, go ahead and talk, right now, you hear?" he says. "But then the boy needs to go with me."

Mama's all upset, but I don't think it's about Casey. "Artie and I need to talk," she says again.

He mumbles something, keeps doing it, and he's walking back and forth.

She says the same thing over and over: "Artie and I need to talk."

Finally he stomps out. He looks at my bike. He grabs it and shoves it in the trunk, and his tires screech when he drives off.

Mama brushes her hair back, and then she reaches for me. I don't like hanging on to her, 'cause I'm too big for that. I'm the man of the house. But I can't let go. She plops down on the couch and sets me on her lap. I touch the place around her eye. It got bigger than at first. She flinches, but she won't tell me to stop. Her face looks different. Maybe she's still losing weight.

"You okay, Mama?"

She nods. "You?"

I can still hear Casey. He's yelling in my head. I can even see him waving that bat.

"Is he coming back, Mama?"

"Not for a while. He's having the same old problems, except they're worse now."

I know something else about that. One of the kids at school was teasing me yesterday. "Cuckoo, hey, cuckoo," he called out on the playground. "Your daddy's cuckoo, and so are you." I took it for a while, then I had to shove him. Somebody ran and told Mrs. Winslow. By the time she got there, we were rolling around hitting each other. She grabbed the other boy, Melvin, and then me, and she took us to the office. I told her what happened, and Melvin got a good talking-to. She sent him home. Then she told me to sit.

"Your father was here earlier today, Artie. He wanted to talk to you."

Oh, man. Mama said he might do that.

"Your mother hired a lawyer," she says. "They went to see a judge. He helped your mother swear out a warrant to keep your father away. Do you understand?"

"Yes'm. Sorta."

"If he shows up here, we'll have to call the police."

"That's okay."

"You're sure?"

"Yes'm."

She got down on one knee and took my hand. "I'll have to tell your mother about it. You just go back to class and learn your lessons."

I took off like a blue streak.

Now Mama rubs her eyes. Kids are still coming by trick and treating, so she lets me watch TV while she passes out some candy. I go to sleep on the couch, with the TV going.

When I wake up, the sun's shining in my face. Mama didn't wake me up for school. She's in the garden. She hasn't done that in a long time. The mustard greens are full of weeds. Some of the stuff is turning brown and getting crinkly. She forgot to pull up the old squash vines, and they shrunk. Bugs ate holes in them, too, and made them look all mealy. She chops them up with this big knife, like she's mad at them. The bean plants are nothing but brown sticks now. She jerks them out and flings them across the yard. Then she tugs on the biggest squash vine. It gives, and she falls down. She throws it, too. She cusses. I never heard her do that before. She turns around. There's dirty stains under her eyes. I have to do something to make it better.

"Come on, Mama, let's make breakfast. You hungry?"

"In a minute." She pulls me down on the wet grass in front of her. I can tell it's more bad news.

"Casey came by the restaurant yesterday."

So that's when he hurt her eye and gave her the poochy lip.

"He caused a big stink. I've been fired, Artie. He'd been hanging around there for a while, yelling. Becky and Bruce said it's bad for business. They can't risk keeping me on, and now I can't afford health insurance. I can't pay the bills."

"But you can get another job." She has to. Papa Merle can't help us. I heard them talking about it.

"It'd be the same thing all over," she says. "Besides, the hours are just too much for me now. The doctor says I need to rest more, and I know he's right. Anyway, Casey's obsessed with having you. He wants you to live with him."

"Mama, no."

"Don't worry, Artie, you won't ever have to. But he thinks he can get regular money from me if he has you. He can still work when he needs to, but he'd rather take the easy way."

"Is he stealing stuff again, Mama?"

"Yes he is, honey," she says. She wipes at the dirty streaks on her face. "And when he can't do that, he comes looking for me. He's losing control, and he's taking it out on us."

"Can't he go to the hospital?" I don't like him at all, not after all the stuff he's done. But I don't want him to be like that.

She jabs the knife in the ground, almost up to the handle. She jerks on it, but it won't come loose. "I'm going to have to go away, Artie. I think I can find work somewhere else, somewhere I can get health insurance and make enough to look after you. But I have to go where Casey can't find me. I'm afraid of him now."

But I don't want to move away. Papa Merle's here. I shake my head real hard.

"I can't take you with me, honey, at least not right now. I won't have a decent place to stay for a while, and you're in school. You're going to have to stay with Papa Merle, at least for the time being."

"But where'll I go to school?" I like Mrs. Winslow and all the teachers. I don't want to go someplace else.

"There's a school, Claxton, in Hillside Park, not far from Grandpa's house. If he can't take you there, you can ride the bus. And if you're still with Papa Merle later, you can go to Asheville High School, down near the hospitals."

High school? I'm just a little kid. I think maybe there's something she's not telling me.

"We're not ever going to be together again, are we?" I say. "You wanna get away from Casey, and me, too."

"No, honey, that's not the way I mean it. It's just that I, Grandpa and I, we have to plan for the unexpected. You do understand, don't you, Artie? I'm having problems, too."

"Besides Casey?"

She won't answer that.

"Please tell me you understand, Artie. I'll die if you and I quit being friends."

Then I put my head in her lap and she rubs my back.

"I'm so sorry, Artie," she says. "I'm so sorry."

All of a sudden I'm mad. I jump up and ball up my fists. "I hate him, Mama! You said he couldn't hurt us, but he's making you go away."

She smiles, but it's a little one. "I'll write you every day. I promise I'll keep stamps and paper and envelopes. Wherever I am, I'll write. I'll try to send Grandpa money once in a while."

We finish talking, and she holds out her arms. I sit on her lap. We don't say a word.

After a while, I think about going to Lake Louise. I want to jump up and get on my bike. Pedal real fast and hear the wind whistle. But I can't do that. My bike's all messed up. The way Papa Merle was looking at it when he left, maybe he can't fix it. But I can get my glove and take off walking. I know I can find some guys to play catch with.

She starts humming. That means she's thinking about something nice. Now I don't care about Lake Louise or playing catch. But I sure hope Papa Merle can fix my bike.

Mama stands up. She pops me on the butt. It's okay, though, 'cause she's playing. "Come on," she says. She heads for the door.

I'm hungry. I bet she is, too.

A. J. — 1988

A cool July breeze slipped down Cullowhee Street and whispered across Merle's long front porch. A.J. rubbed a sprinkling of goose bumps from his arms, rose from his seat on the steps. Since coming to live with his great-grandfather, Merle, A.J. had grown into a slightly darker, more muscular and taller version of his father, Casey. He leaped to the gravel drive and searched out a patch of sky between the oaks. The clouds had moved southward, the electric smell of summer rain gone. Good. The fireworks show would happen after all, and Sandy was on the way.

"When's she gonna get here?" Merle called out.

A.J. turned, watched the old man fan a gnarled hand at some unseen thing. A nearby dove added its hollow phrasings to the porch floor's creaks as Merle slumped back in his rocker.

"Anytime now."

"This shirt I got on, it's a little messy." Merle bent forward, shuffled his brogans. "Don't want her thinking your Papa Merle's messy."

A.J. huffed, said nothing.

"Sure do like that little girl."

A.J. jammed a hand deep into a jeans pocket, felt the ring at the bottom. He raked a sneaker through the gravel. If he were to try orchestrating a good impression for a rich girl like Sandy, it'd take more than a clean shirt on Merle.

For starters, he'd make this old house disappear. Everywhere he looked, embarrassment loomed. Grass and weeds stood a foot high. Merle had long since abandoned the shrubs to a swirl of vines. Lumpy, hundred year-old oaks standing between house and street were in desperate need of pruning. The roof's wooden shingles were split and rotting. Gutters hung limply, still drooling from the afternoon rain. A green scum had added its blight to the porch's once-white columns. Inside, the house seemed a dungeon of gloom, the ancient wallpaper and trim painted over in too-dark yellows and browns. Even the windowpanes had grown dim and foreboding with years of accumulated grime.

A.J. shook his head, bemused. Sandy had shown no sign of revulsion when she'd first visited. In fact, she'd seemed okay with the run-down property, the dingy house. Didn't even flinch when she'd met smelly old Merle. A.J. straightened from his usual slouch. Then he glanced to his frayed, too-short jeans, thought about changing his own shirt. But his other three were as worn as this one. A pensive sigh. Pretty soon, though, I'll be out of here, away from Merle and his battle fatigue, his booze, his stinking poverty. It'll take a while, then it'll be just Sandy and me.

At first, he'd taken to Merle's company, even to the chores. He'd swept floors and Merle had mopped. He'd mowed and raked while Merle had hewed the hedges into a roughly ordered look. He'd dried the dishes the old man had washed, and he'd folded clothes with him at the Laundromat. Merle had even taught him a little carpentry. At night, the old man had led him through all the Nova Scotia dances, told and retold his Acadian stories, even tried to teach him how to fiddle.

A.J. peered up the street. One of the neighbors' boys, Jeffrey something, rumbled into his family's driveway in a ragtop Jeep, sound system blaring. This kid'll be a sophomore at Asheville High next year, A.J. grumbled, and he already has a car. A new one at that. A.J. could only frown in envy.

In the weeks since A.J. had graduated from Asheville High, Sandy had been his savior from Merle's shabby world. During their last high school year, she'd driven him home every day from school and baseball practice. They'd done their homework together. At graduation, she'd wolf-whistled during his Salutatorian introduction, causing waves of laughter among the seniors. He'd blushed and grinned, but had managed to negotiate his brief speech. Now, Sandy's summer job at the Citizen-Times newspaper filled her days, with only Merle to fill A.J.'s.

A.J. had done well in the classroom and on the SATs, but hadn't won the academic scholarship he'd hoped for. Extra-curricular credentials would've helped make his case, but he'd missed out there, too—except for baseball. *I should've taken Casey's advice, focused more on the game,* he grumped. That dubious bit of encouragement had come not long after Casey and A.J.'s mother, Marie, had divorced and Casey had wound up in jail. *If I'd have worked harder on baseball, maybe I'd have had a better chance for that athletic scholarship.* UNC scouts had come in April of his senior year, had given him a casual look, then left. *No, I had to waste my time taking care of Merle and dancing to that scratchy fiddle.*

He glanced back to the old man. "Hey, Merle!"

Merle's head had arced toward his chest—his afternoon psychiatric meds had kicked in. For all the good they did.

"Merle!"

Merle jerked awake, ran a finger under his nose, sniffed, looked up.

"Merle," A.J. called out. "Go ahead, now, okay? Put on that other shirt."

Merle nodded. "I'm gonna enjoy this breeze a little bit first."

"Don't forget, okay?"

Even during his and Merle's first years together, A.J. had noted the old man wasn't bathing and shaving regularly, was wearing the same clothes for days on end. Then Merle's nightmares had begun. So many times, A.J. had risen deep in the night as Merle bellowed in terror, had fixed the old man a stiff drink and collapsed into a bedside chair while he waited for the booze to take.

Even so, there had been some good times. The old man had watched him pitch for a season in Little League. He'd taken A.J. to baseball games at McCormick Field, out to eat once a week, even to an occasional movie. After three years together, and to Merle's delight, A.J. had begun interrupting the old man's stories to embellish on them. In the next few years, the pair had swapped delightful, far-fetched lies as they tended sporadically to their chores, made occasional house repairs and tinkered with Merle's ancient Buick.

But their once-a-week dinners had fallen by the wayside, as had the baseball games and movies. The music and lie swapping, the shared chores, these too had atrophied and fallen away as Merle surrendered in incoherent fright to his World War II nightmares.

That had meant making excuses for the old man, something pre-teen A.J. had hated. Merle had been a gregarious presence in the neighborhood, and to A.J. it seemed he knew everyone for blocks around. So as Merle's health had soured, neighborhood friends continued to stop by. "Papa Merle didn't sleep well last night," A.J. would tell them over and over, the old man hungover and mumbling to himself in his darkened bedroom. Sometimes, so the excuses might take on a more believable cast, he'd tell them, "Merle stayed up late fiddling. He's napping now." Soon they'd understood that Merle wasn't fit company and had quit coming.

In January of A.J.'s senior year, the school secretary had called him to the principal's office. Mr. Macadam, the principal, buttoned his suit coat, smiled, and extended a hand. A.J. took it, surprised at the strength of the principal's grip.

"Thanks for coming," Macadam said. "It's Arthur, isn't it?"

"A.J." He let the man's hand go and edged back a step, wondering: Am I in trouble?

"You've finally taken to your studies, the way we all knew you could," Macadam said. "Your I.Q. is quite high, did you know that?"

"No, sir."

Macadam nodded. "Well. No matter. I just wanted to congratulate you on your report cards this year. All As, I'm told."

"Right," said A.J. "Yes, sir."

"Your parents must be very supportive."

A.J. got it then. He thinks my folks made me knuckle down, do my homework. He resisted the cynical smile he felt coming. Didn't Macadam read my file? Doesn't he know my situation?

"I'd like to meet your parents. Do you think they can drop by, say, Wednesday, about three?"

Right, thought A.J. now as he scratched at his first blond chin stubble. He'd declined as tactfully as he could manage, telling the principal that he lived with his grandfather, who was ailing and couldn't leave the house—a merely distorted truth.

And Merle's mental deterioration had made life awkward in other ways. A.J. kicked at the stony drive again, burying his sneaker toe deep in it and sending a clattering spray into the bushes. A blue jay protested and fluttered away. With no opportunity to get a driver's license, he'd been forced to ride his decrepit child's bike to high school games he'd pitched in. His teammates had driven, most of them in new cars. Seeing them with cell phones, cars, and new clothes while I make do with Merle's nothing... Such thoughts always tailed off to embarrassment. He'd felt set apart from his teammates, even from the "brains," the ones he had the most in common with. Then something good had happened. He'd met Sandy.

It had been the final month of his junior year, and he was pitching Asheville High's last game. He'd allowed men to reach first and third. With two outs in the fifth, his catcher trotted to the mound.

"How's your hand?" Tom, the catcher, asked.

"Blisters." A.J. rubbed the first two fingers on his left hand with the thumb.

"Coach said tell you this guy can't hit a curve. Jam him with your heater, then show him the deuce."

A.J. nodded.

Tom glanced toward the first base bleachers. "Oh, that babe with the long brown hair? She's been asking some of the guys about you. I think she wants you to know. Name's Sandy."

He followed Tom's nod to the bleachers, found her.

Tom grinned. "You don't talk to her, I will."

A.J. struck the batter out on four pitches, the curve bursting one of his blisters. Trotting to the dugout, he made eye contact with Sandy and smiled. They talked.

"Want to do something?" she asked. "Where're you parked?"

He managed to avoid glancing at his old bike, chained to a nearby post. He looked to the open blister and mumbled, "I got a ride with Tom."

"You can ride with me."

On that, their first date, they ate burgers in a noisy café in Biltmore Village. Sandy paid.

During their school lunch hours together, she gently probed his past and, after a sullen resistance, he began to bare his skeletons. She listened to his Merle stories, the bitter reminiscences of a troubled, criminal father, a gone but not forgotten mother. Sandy had teared up as A.J. had told his stories, and then so had he. She'd taken his hand in both of hers. With that, his woes had shrunk to nothing.

At last—he'd regained the sounding board, the confidante he'd once had in Marie. With Sandy in his life, he no longer had to try wringing emotional support from Merle. For the first time, he'd begun openly to resent the old man's disease, his slovenliness, the hardships he'd drawn A.J. into. They'd begun to argue.

One day he told Sandy, "I'm thinking about quitting school. Move out, get a job."

"Don't," she counseled, "he's all you have left."

"No," he said, "I have you."

Without her, he considered as he paced the drive, I wouldn't have had the guts to leave here, do something with my life. I'd have died a slow death tied to Merle.

The whine of a car engine grew louder. The black '65 Mustang convertible Sandy's father had restored and given to her at the beginning of her junior year turned between the crumbling rubblework columns and up the drive.

He met her halfway, leaned in and kissed her. Damn, she smelled good. A trace of perfume rose from her neck, taking away what was left of his breath. She wore a man's crimson dress shirt, probably one her brother Charlie had given her as he left Harvard for New York. She wore it with two buttons open at the top, the pockets swollen over mature breasts, the shirttails tied high on her midriff. The tight, tanned abdomen dropping to the top of her white shorts, the flare of her hips—that sight always made him ache. Eyeing him mischievously, she slid under the steering wheel, legs wide, her shorts taut.

His knees almost buckled. With any other girl, he would've considered this display trashy. But to him, she was just being competitive, showing him she was the pick of the lot around town, that she wanted him to want her, only her.

Two other girls had stalked A.J. in the school's halls during senior year, something Sandy had been aware of. He'd been flattered, even spent time between classes talking to the two. Every time that happened, though, Sandy would appear, and the other girls would smile sweetly and edge away.

Now, in thrall to her smoky blue eyes, perplexity took him again. Whatever made her interested in a poor guy like me in the first place? Well, it hardly matters. She loves me, she told me so.

But something else added to his perplexity; he had to blink to keep from seeing his mother Marie in her. Tender. Attentive, doting. She even looked vaguely like Marie. She's so much more, though, he thought, once again fighting the Oedipal transposition. He adjusted his jeans and bent at the waist in hopes that the aching he projected wasn't too obvious. He took her hand.

"Let me go, baby," she said. "I want to say hello to Merle."

His hand slid away, and he forced his eyes from her, toward the porch. "I wouldn't get too close. He hasn't taken a bath."

"How're the spells?"

"Hard to tell. He never lets on when he's about to go off the deep end, just starts babbling."

"Is that a bottle?" She had leaned forward, looking through the dimming light to Merle's rocker.

A.J. nodded. "Drinks most of the time."

She eased out the clutch and the Mustang's tires crunched across the gravel. A.J. turned to the sagging garage for his bike. Stepping inside, he pulled the ring from his pocket, lifted it to the faint light. Eighteen carat gold, the man had told him, with a diamond set in it. Looks pretty grand to me, even though you have to squint to see the diamond. He let out a long breath as he thought about what he'd done. He'd robbed Merle. But I don't care. He'll never miss the medals now.

That morning, he'd gone through Merle's footlocker, typical of those issued to soldiers prior to World War II. The contents were a filthy, scrambled mess, but A.J. had found the medals wrapped in a tattered undershirt and had shoved them into a plastic grocery bag. Merle was asleep on the porch, so A.J. eased out the back door, cut across Mrs. Haskins' yard and walked to a pawnshop on Merrimon Avenue.

The business occupied a third of an old brick building: a long, narrow room with a high, plastered ceiling, a random pattern of stains betraying roof leaks. The place exuded a musty smell. A slant of morning sun fell on settling dust, adding a glow to the shop's contents. Behind a long glass display case, guitars and fiddles hung in a row above a small array of mini TVs, computers, and electric appliances. At the end nearest the entrance, a collection of antique pistols lay under glass on the case's bare oak base. From the middle to the far end, a broad swath of men's and women's jewelry beckoned.

The proprietor, a short, bald man with a sagging belly and the sideways limp of one wearing an old-fashioned leg prosthesis, eyed him. "Help you?"

A.J. pulled his bundle from the bag and showed him the medals. "You interested in these?"

The man picked through them with one finger. "Where'd you get these?"

"My great-grandpa's. They're a wedding gift to me and my fiancée."

The man picked up each of the ten medals, held them to the light, turned them over, set them in a neat row on the case's glass top. "Two Purple Hearts. Wounded, huh?"

"Yep, invading France. The others are campaign medals, I think, and then a bunch of ribbons."

The man pointed to a green ribbon with gold stripes and tiny brass add-ons, then a similar yellow one. "These are commendations." He pointed to the green one. "Three oak leaf clusters. The old fella must've been something."

Sadness rose in A.J. with the man's comment. For a moment, guilt engulfed him. Then he bent across the display case. "Look," he said, "I need an engagement ring, and these medals are all I have."

The man sniffed, pulled a small spiral pad from the pocket of his yellowed shirt, made some notes. "Give you fifty dollars," he said. "Not much of a market for these. Only one or two local collectors."

A.J. had been peering at a line of rings under the glass as the man had evaluated the medals. "If you'll let me have that ring for the fifty."

The man searched out the one A.J. wanted, scratched his shiny head. "Need to get one-fifty for that, son."

A.J. stiffened. He was going to have to bargain. "Come on, now," he said, puffing out his chest in his best imitation of Merle, "you can get two-fifty for those medals, easy."

The man frowned. "I got to make a living." Then his expression grew soft. "I lost my leg in Korea, on

Heartbreak Ridge. Your great-grandpa, did he come home whole?"

"He came back with all his parts, but now he's losing his mind. He dreams about the war all the time."

The shopkeeper sniffed. "Well, since he was wounded, and you're getting married and all, I guess just this once I can take a hit on something."

"An even trade?"

The man had sighed and nodded

A.J. stuffed the ring back in his pocket, peered into the garage's murk for his bike, found it leaning against a wall below a dingy window. He rummaged, pulled a rag from a pile of old clothes atop a discarded chest of drawers, where he'd stashed a trove of Marie's letters. He slapped dust and spider webs from the bike. Then he lifted it and pressed a thumb into each tire. Good—air pressure was still fine.

Its blue paint had been flaking for years, exposing the original red Merle had found offensive, saying it reminded him of France and the war. Merle had brought the bike with Marie's things when he'd moved her into the old house. That had been in 'seventy-one, after a stroke had taken A.J.'s grandmother Martha, soon after Jeremiah, A.J.'s grandfather, had died in Vietnam. That had been a year prior to Marie and Casey's marriage. "Got to get rid of that color, Marie," Merle had told her. "Don't need nothing looks so much like blood 'round here." So Merle had bought a couple of cans of blue spray paint and had covered the red.

A.J had researched the bike a year or so earlier from a computer at the Asheville High library. A boy's, called an Apple Krate, named for its original red color. The serial number had revealed its origin, circa 1968, selling for a then-expensive ninety dollars. If in mint condition now, it would bring close to two thousand from a collector.

He let out a sour grunt and stood the bike on the garage's cracked concrete floor. Mint condition? Not even close, just like everything else around here. The chrome was pitted, the long Springer seat cracked and misshapen. The stickshift worked only occasionally, barely well enough to navigate nearby streets in north Asheville. Tonight it'd be fine, he figured; no long ride would be involved. They'd drive down Asheland to a medical facility parking lot and ride to a spot near McCormick Field to watch the post-baseball fireworks.

Sandy had found a dual rack to fit the Mustang's trunk lid, and her bike was already attached. He set his on the brackets above hers, fastened it, shook it. Then he plodded toward the porch, where Merle was gazing past Sandy, as if peering into another time.

"Woulda stayed on the water all year if I could," Merle was saying, "but those Nova Scotia winters, they chase you in."

Sandy smiled. "You couldn't get out much at all, huh? Those long nights must've dragged by."

Merle looked her way, chuckled hoarsely, wagged a stubby finger. "They wasn't so bad as you make out, little girl. We always made 'em go by, hardly had one idle hour. Most of the time, we tied nets and overhauled boats.

Sometimes it'd warm up some, and we'd go hunting. When the storms went real long, though, we carved. The whole dang inside of the house looked like a totem pole." His laughter rose to a volume A.J. hadn't heard in years.

Somewhere in the overgrown yard, crickets began their songs, punctuated by a tree frog pair's back-and-forth.

"We just tried to stay warm," Merle went on. "But before the snows came, I always made a point of taking off upcountry. Cape Breton, the mountains up there. That's where I learned the fiddle." He paused, again peering into his past. "Fiddling, that's what got me by."

"You're going to play some for us tonight, aren't you, Merle?"

"Sure, hon. You come back 'fore I get sleepy, I'll play a little bit."

"Don't get drunk, then," said A.J. "You don't play worth a shit when you're drunk. You sound like cats howling."

Merle sniffed, eyed Sandy. "That boy friend of yours, he's got a bad mouth. Takes after his daddy with that."

She turned to hide her smile.

"See if you can teach him some manners, huh, little girl? I sure can't do nothing with him."

"He's fine, Merle, just concerned with your health, that's all."

The old man settled back, eyes closed, fingers curved over his belly, scratched the exposed flesh between his shirt buttons. "Go on, now, have some fun. That's what young folks supposed to do."

She bent, kissed Merle's whiskery cheek. He grinned, brogans pawing back and forth. Then she took A.J.'s hand, and they clumped down the porch steps.

"I get my fiddle," Merle called out. "Tune it up just right. We can dance a little bit."

A.J. took the rider's seat. Sandy laughed as she started the car. "Can't you make him take off those filthy clothes, maybe wash him down in the yard?"

"You didn't have to get close enough to kiss him."

She glanced, reached for his hand. He pressed hers, let go.

"He needs a little affection, that's all," she said.

On Cullowhee, she gunned the engine. The Mustang's tires barked. At Montford, she downshifted, and the Mustang's rear end slid with the hard left turn, tires screeching.

That was a quirk counterpointing her soft, giving nature, something to make A.J. forget his barely concealed jealousy at her attention to Merle: she was determined to make her presence known. He pictured her at school—all poise and beauty. But out here on the streets she wanted to make noise. Maybe it's that well-off upbringing, he thought. Maybe she needs to leave skid marks on my world because she isn't allowed to do that on hers. He sighed softly. Or maybe she's just slumming, and making her tires howl is part of that.

The tiny hummingbird she'd had tattooed on one buttock? Maybe that's slumming, too. When her mom had found out, she'd raged at what she called one more instance of Sandy's teenaged stupidity. A.J. smiled, remembered mentioning the episode to Merle on one of his more lucid days. "Sonny boy," Merle had laughed, "that's just growing pains."

She was to attend UNC-Chapel Hill in the fall and major in journalism. With an eye on television, she harbored dreams of becoming the next Christiane Amanpour. She'd show the world, she told A.J., especially her mom, that she wasn't going to become a bejeweled, flawlessly coiffed ornament-cum-baby machine for some rich, bratty Asheville boy.

Then his vision turned inward, to Marie. He tried to shoo away his mother's haunting presence, but he couldn't. He'd long ago realized Marie hadn't just left him temporarily in Merle's hands, she'd abandoned him. Not the way Casey had, but she'd abandoned him all the same. At first, she'd been true to her word, had written him faithfully, every other day for two years, had sent dribs and drabs of money to Merle. Letters arrived from Charlotte, then Raleigh, then Wilmington, Charleston, Atlanta, Jacksonville, Miami, Mobile, Biloxi, New Orleans, and Houston. The letters became shorter, less communicative, and he began to cry in his room as he read the half-empty pages.

One day she'd showed up in a rusty Cadillac with a longhaired man named Lou. She held a long conversation with Merle. Afterward, she knocked at A.J.'s door, closed it, sat beside him on the bed.

The thirteen-year-old pushed away. "Who's that man?"

"A friend, that's all." Marie moved closer. She'd lost a lot of weight, her face gaunt, her long brown hair fairing to a premature gray. "I guess I haven't been a good mother lately, have I?"

"No'm."

"I'm really sorry, Artie."

"A.J. I'm A.J. now."

She took his hand. "Grandpa told me."

"I don't like it, though. He wanted me to quit being a Royal, change to Jongleur. But we finally settled it, so now it's A.J. Arthur Jongleur Royal."

"Well, that's between you and Grandpa."

He squirmed away from her. "Why'd you come?"

She sat primly before him. "I have something important to talk to you about. I'm sick, A.J., very sick."

He looked to the faded wallpaper. "You're gonna die."

"I'm so sorry."

During his darkest moments, when he'd missed her the most, he'd thought of her cramps, her weight loss, had wondered in the months between her later letters whether she was sick, really sick. She was, he'd convinced himself, and that was why she'd stopped writing altogether. But hearing it face to face was too much.

"That's why I haven't written much lately." Marie said. "I didn't want to tell you about it."

He could think of nothing to say to her. Then anger flared. *She's sorry,* he thought. *Yeah, right. And now she's gonna leave me again.*

"I have cancer," she went on. "It's been with me for a long while. I had to move from place to place to keep finding decent jobs, ones that would help me pay my medical bills. I had treatments. I lost my hair from them, lost more weight, too. It was with me before you came to stay with Grandpa. If I'd had it diagnosed earlier, had better treatment, maybe I could've beaten it."

"You could've stayed. I would've taken care of you."

One tear followed another down her hollow cheeks. She pulled him to her. She held him the way she used to, his sobs muffled in her skeletal chest.

After he'd quieted, she said, "I know you would've helped me, honey. So would Grandpa, if I'd asked. But it wouldn't have been fair to either of you. The whole thing made me depressed, and I didn't want to be a burden. Anyway, I just had to be by myself, make peace with it, you know, before the end came."

He blinked, nodded that he understood. But he didn't. So many of these adult things still eluded his young mind.

"There's this hospital in New Orleans for people with terminal illnesses. In a couple of days, I'm going back, going to work there until I can't anymore, then I'll be a patient."

"Until you die."

"Yes, until then."

"You going to write?"

"Every chance I get."

For a while, neither spoke. Marie held him close, rocked him sideways at the bed's edge.

Finally, he squirmed free. "You know Papa Merle's bad off."

"He's old, A.J. The war, those experiences, they were bound to get to him sooner or later. Will you look after him? Until he's gone?"

"I s'pose."

"He didn't have to, but he took me in, the way he did you. He's had a hard time of it for years and years. Promise me you'll look after him."

"Yes'm." He would, because she'd made him promise, but he didn't want to. He wanted to be like other boys, free from such terrible responsibilities.

"If you'll do that, when he's gone, then you can go, A.J. You can do whatever you want with your life. That's what Grandpa would want, and me, and Casey, too."

She left with Lou, waving from the Caddy, and that had been the last time he'd seen her. She did write a few times from New Orleans. He found out about her death a month after the fact, when Merle showed him her death certificate, ovarian cancer the cause.

From that moment, he began transferring his anger at Casey and Marie to Merle. As he watched Merle grow weaker and more disturbed, he plotted his getaway. He'd study hard, get good grades in case he had a chance for a college scholarship. He'd stay out of trouble. And he'd grow up, as quickly as he could. He'd be ready when Merle was gone. But as his high school years had passed, he'd grown more impatient, more claustrophobic. When school's over, he'd resolved, whether Merle's alive or not, I'm leaving.

A Navy recruiter had come to Asheville High. A.J. had listened to his spiel, the descriptions of shipboard life, exotic foreign ports, an expanse of water reaching in all directions beyond the horizon. An ocean. Yeah, that'll do it. He'd never seen an ocean, but hearing this chief petty officer describe it, the seas had taken on mystical proportions. A body of water half a world wide. Wow! A wild, dangerous, enthralling presence, something humans couldn't tame or shape to their desires.

Maybe it was Merle's tales of fishing in the North Atlantic that had opened him to the idea, but he'd decided he'd even give up what was left of his baseball dreams for the Navy. He needed what this recruiter offered—at least for awhile—a life so unlike that in these mountains, with no confining history. In the Navy he'd have the distance he needed from his past, the family that had left him, shamed him. If he made it through boot camp he'd willingly take any billet they assigned. He was a quick study; he'd learn. When the opportunity presented itself, he'd apply to Officer Candidate School. He'd learn to lead. He'd learn naval tactics. After that, he'd be prepared for anything, maybe even the next big war. Maybe he'd retire an Admiral, Sandy standing proudly at his side.

So the week of graduation, he'd signed up.

Now he leaned to the right, let the wind wash away Sandy's Van Halen music. Street noise took his attention, then the muffled thump of firecrackers somewhere nearby.

He hoped he hadn't waited too long. He had to ask her to marry him, and soon. So far, they'd made no real plans, no promises. He had to say his piece, before he caught that bus to boot camp. He had to.

Sandy slipped the Mustang onto a side street, found a parking space, pulled a backpack from behind the driver's seat. A.J. unfastened his bike and hers, a jealous pang of another sort jolting him as he stood them. Hers was lean and elegant, built for street speed, his a scruffy child's bike.

She'd offered to buy him a new one for his birthday back in January, but he'd refused, just as he'd refused the college loan her father had offered just last week.

Her father was a pleasant sort, but sometimes a bit standoffish. A.J. had walked on eggshells around the man, figuring he was simply indulging Sandy's first, long-term romantic involvement. So the tuition offer had been a shock. And A.J. had surprised himself with his refusal, even after the father had promised the tuition would be there when A.J. got out of the Navy.

By A.J.'s reasoning, he couldn't take the gift bike any more than the loan. He'd lost Casey, then Marie, Merle a shell of his old, extroverted self. The ratty blue bike was all he had left. No, it was more than a possession, it was the last connection to stability, his family, his childhood. He'd keep it in Merle's garage until he was through with the Navy, maybe restore it someday. And the loan. That offer had seemed a threat to his future independence, something else he treasured and had resolved to protect.

Sandy straddled her bike. A.J. tested his brakes, tugged on the stickshift. Everything seemed in working order, for now.

"Which way?" she asked.

"Let's head back north. We can see better from there."

They rode east on Southside and north up Charlotte Street, the main thoroughfare between McCormick Field and the Interstate. A.J. sweated as the bike labored from grade to grade. He'd underestimated the distance he could pedal the old bike before fatigue claimed him. Damned thing. It was too hard to pedal, his long legs bent, knees skewering side space. Now the stickshift was working only in low gear.

From her half-block lead, Sandy looked back, slowed, waggled her front wheel, waited. He pedaled hard, panted, sweat in his eyes. A long block later, they stopped, let their bikes fall to the grass off the sidewalk.

She tossed him a hand towel, took a blanket from her backpack, then a pair of sandwiches. She drew out two cans of still-cool soft drinks and a small radio.

A.J. wiped away his sweat, tuned to the game, in the eighth inning, the Class A Tourists ahead by four. A half-inning to go.

Someone nearby turned on a blaster box, playing rowdy country music. Three young couples began dancing on the walk, so A.J. and Sandy danced, too. The tempo changed without interruption to a slow, country waltz.

"Slow dance?" Sandy asked.

He nodded, took her hand. She moved with him in spiraling steps down the walk. She'd taught him this dance, and God, he loved doing it with her. It was as if they were one thing, free and flowing, high above the ordinary. In mid-song, he stopped, sighed, lifted her chin with a crooked finger.

"What?" Her beautiful face flushed with curiosity and excitement.

The practiced words caught in his throat. Maybe it'd be too big a shock, he thought. Maybe we need to talk about the big picture first, about where we're both going, when we'll be able to get together for real, for good.

"Later," he whispered.

A cheer went up, and someone yelled. The Tourists had won. Sandy and A.J. reclaimed their place off the sidewalk and began eating. Then a faint roar sounded. The radio announcer proclaimed the Independence Day celebration begun.

Sandy pulled a flask from the pack, poured bourbon into their drink cans. "Enough?"

He tasted. It was too much, but he wasn't going to complain. They'd get mildly drunk, he figured. Just enough to push his anxieties to the background. Then he'd propose.

The first thump came, then another, and another. The distant sky exploded in a burst of reds and yellows and hues too ethereal to discern. They oohed together.

Sandy shifted closer. A.J. moved a leg to encircle her. She was sweating a little from drink and humidity.

A banshee whistle echoed to announce another explosion, this one setting off fractured globes of color. As they watched, his hands slipped upward. He felt the rise and fall of her breathing.

Then a rat-a-tat echoed in the distance, and the sky surrendered to streams of brilliance, rising, then arching, falling. They whistled, clapped, fell laughing against the cooling grass. She rolled into his arms and they kissed. Sitting up, she took his hand in both hers, and bent to his ear. "Artie."

She insisted on calling him that, despite his dislike for it. It was a child's name, one he'd outgrown, his preference Art, even A.J.

"Artie," she said, "let's go back to your place. Let's do it, okay? I really need it tonight. You want to, don't you, isn't that what you wanted to ask me?"

He nodded, the yeah, sure, you bet, caught in his throat. That would be the perfect time, after they'd made love, then he'd give her the ring. He rose, helped her up, and without a word they gathered their things and mounted the bikes.

As Sandy started the Mustang and drove off, he clamped his hands about his knees. That would help him stay alert as she dodged with characteristic abandon through traffic. But Marie came again, stole his view of the road. Those thoughts led him back to a time just before she'd left, her knees to the ground, weeding what was left of their vegetable garden. "You're on nature's clock when you tend a garden," she'd said. "You have to be there when it needs you, not when you feel like it." Then her tone had changed, insistent, telling him to take it slow with Sandy. "You have responsibilities. The last Jongleur needs you.

Remember your promise? Take care of Merle. When he's gone you can go, too."

The car ground to a stop on the driveway gravel. Then a voice from the porch, high-pitched and quivering.

"That's Merle?"

A.J. nodded. "The fireworks probably set him off. It was like this last year."

They swung from their seats, clicked the car doors shut. A.J. returned his bike to the garage, and they crept up the porch stairs. The fiddle lay across Merle's lap, bow in his right hand, dangling over the rocker's arm to the floor. He stirred, began to babble in two distinctive voices.

A.J. stooped, lifted the fiddle from the old man's lap, eased the bow from his hand, placed both in the case, snapped it shut. "Come on," he whispered.

Together he and Sandy edged through the dark. The high foyer ceiling's wallpaper sheets had come unglued at the top. They fluttered gently with the house's air currents, creating ghostly shadows. At the foot of the stairs, A.J. and Sandy separated, hands on the banister, felt their way up. From the landing, they groped across groaning floorboards to his room.

She closed the door, turned on a tiny desk lamp. He lifted a square floor fan to the window, nudged it into place, turned the switch. The room's stale smell thinned, then cleared. The humid night, the bike ride, and the bourbon had left him hot and sticky, and the fan helped take away this unclean feeling. Lost in its drone, he rubbed away as much of the stickiness as he could with his shirttail. Then he leaned over the fan and listened for a while to Merle's faint yammering.

"Artie!" Sandy tugged his arm. "Artie, what's the matter?"

"Merle," he said, "he gets to me, that's all."

"It's okay, baby, it's okay."

She pulled at his buttons and his sodden shirt fell away. They fell naked to his narrow bed, the sheets cooling for a moment, fan humming on the other side of the room, Merle's faint voice rising, falling. A.J. lost himself in her, in the warm wetness that drove him crazy, pushing and pulling him into sensations, emotions, he'd never imagined before her. Finally, they collapsed, intertwined, and fell asleep.

The bedside clock read early morning. A.J. groaned. Sandy snuggled into him, woke, swung a leg over his, ran a hand in soft circles across his chest.

"It's after one," he whispered.

She reached down, raked a finger along the inside of his leg. He wriggled, stiffened. She was ready again. He thought once more of the ring, of their need to talk things out. But this was a different moment, and in this one she wasn't the totality of his world.

"I need to see about Merle," he whispered. Lifting her hand away, he rose, pulled on his jeans. She sighed, swung to the bed's edge, began dressing.

He watched her in the dim light, her bare skin, her shape drawing him as if a magnet, even after all this. He opened his mouth, ready to ask her. Again he couldn't. He felt the ring, its firmness, pressed it hard to the pocket's bottom.

They crept down the stairs to the porch. A.J. knelt, shook Merle roughly. The old man woke with a grunt, kicked over a half-full bottle of Jim Beam. The contents glugged away and began to drip between the withered porch boards to the dirt.

Merle blinked, looked to A.J., then Sandy. "You two been upstairs again," he said, "doing what young folks do."

A.J. flushed. "How would you know what we've been doing, Merle? You've been off in France."

Sandy bent, rubbed the back of Merle's neck. "It was like you were two different people."

"Yeah." Merle nodded. "It was France, all right, I remember now. Sometimes Jerry come with me, too. He help me flush out fascists."

A.J. eyed him, confused. "Grandpa Jerry?"

Merle nodded again. "We got a bond. He come in my dreams, just like that. Help out."

A.J. laughed, trying to mock, but the laughter dribbled out in uneasy spasms.

Merle rubbed his face, eyes closed, felt his lap for the fiddle. "You don't understand, do you, sonny boy? Who says we ain't all hooked together like a string o'pearls, one thing together, no matter what?"

A. J. jostled him. "Come on now, let's get you to bed. Sleep until noon, if you want to, but let go of all this."

With effort, Merle screwed his flaccid face into a frown. "Leave me be, son." He groped sideways, reached for the porch floor. "Where my fiddle?"

"Inside the door."

"Let me have it. Need to fiddle."

A.J. nodded to Sandy, who reached for the case, opened it, handed Merle the instrument and bow. Then she bent, kissed the old man.

A.J followed her to the car.

She leaned against the Mustang's door, reached a hand to A.J.'s cheek. "You're tired."

"Worried."

"Worried? Why?"

He fished the ring from his pocket, held it between them. "Because I don't know if you'll want this."

She peered at it, gave him a wondering look, and then the ring's significance dawned.

"I-I want us to be married," he stammered. "So we can be together, forever."

She looked down for a moment, placed a hand on her bare midriff. "Now, Artie? Before the Navy?"

He nodded.

"Why now?"

His mouth was dry; this wasn't going according to script. "We might let it go if we don't."

She kissed him, shook her head. "Not now. There's...well, I can't."

He pushed away, frowned.

"Not now," she said, shaking her head emphatically. "Not now, Artie."

"I-I don't understand."

"I can't keep you from doing what you need to do." Her face contorted. "We could've—" She stifled a sob. "Why'd you have to join the Navy?"

A.J. swallowed. She was rejecting him, not for any good reason, but because things hadn't gone her way. "Tell the truth," he said, voice rising. "You're dumping me."

She shook her head.

"You don't give a damn about me," he said, louder.

Her mouth opened, then she pressed a hand to it. She seemed about to tell him something. Then she turned, climbed into the Mustang, and screeched off.

He balled his fists to fight back anger. One thing he'd learned, and learned well—he couldn't have it all. Okay, I'm an adult now, by most people's standards. Take it like a man. Get on with your life, Art.

He mounted the steps, patted Merle's shoulder. Even in the dark, he could make out the old man's eyes-closed smile as he drew his bow across the out-of-tune strings, filling the instrument's void with a discordant, melancholic music.

"Get some sleep, Merle, okay?"

The old man's smile broadened, the request unacknowledged. A.J.'s heart suddenly ached, a lump in his throat. They'd had good times, and bleak ones, but Merle had always been there. Now I have to leave him, the way Casey and Marie left me. He plodded up the stairs and to his room, sat on the bed, head in hands. From the porch, Merle's discordant melody rose and fell in waves, searching for some elusive repose.

A.J. woke. The night sky had faded to pale morning gray. He smelled smoke. Pulling the fan from the window, he looked down. A few bold flames were licking at the morning air from the garage, red and yellow and blue, vigorous, leaping. A black gauze hovered inside the sagging structure, swelling, oozing out and up, diffusing among the oaks. Merle stood facing the fire, bow dragging the ground. He was babbling. Then he drew the bow up, aimed it as if it were the M-1 rifle he'd once carried.

"Sniper!" he yelled, the bow arcing from tree to tree. "See him? There! Get 'im!" He hobbled to the garage, turned, brought the bow to port arms, stared open-mouthed into the branches of an adjacent tree. After a few seconds, his chin fell slack and he began mumbling again, oblivious to the flames.

A.J. bounded down the stairs, taking them three at a time, naked except for his underpants, out the front door, onto the drive, gravel bruising his feet. He grabbed Merle by his scorched shirt, jerked him from the fire.

Merle tugged away. "Damn it, Lieuten't, geddown. You wan' get shot?"

"It's A.J., Merle," he yelled. He grabbed Merle's broad shoulders, shook his sagging bulk. "You're home, Merle, you're home."

Merle blinked, mumbled something. "Snipers," he said, eyes blank, staring into nothingness.

"No snipers. Just me and you." A.J. shook him again. "Come on, you're getting burned."

Merle turned a sneer to A.J. "C'llaborators. Fascist c'llaborators. Smoke 'em out. Smoke 'em out."

A.J. slapped him, hard. "Goddamn it, Merle, you set the garage on fire. Get in the house."

"Garage?" Merle's shoulders slumped forward. He gave to the tugging, allowed A.J. to lead him from the fire. Then he licked his lips. "Need a drink."

"I'll get some water, your tranquilizer, too. Stay here. Promise me you'll stay here."

Merle nodded, licked his dry, faceted lips.

A.J. leaped onto the porch, ran to the kitchen, dialed, gave the fire station the address, a hurried description of the garage, the fire. Then he ran to Merle's room, found his pills, returned to the kitchen, ran a glass of water.

On the gravel again, he turned, searching. "Merle!" he yelled. "Merle!"

No answer.

He raced to the garage, saw a shadowy figure inside. No! He threw the pill and water into the weeds, took a breath, and plunged in.

Merle had moved deep inside, toward the nearest window. A.J saw him pulling at something. The chest of drawers where A.J. had stowed Marie's letters. Fire danced across the chest's top, devouring its shellacked finish, the dry wood barking as it shriveled and split. Merle staggered back. The chest crashed to the floor in an explosion of sparks.

A.J. leaped away, rubbed his arms, dancing to avoid coals and flames. Merle had moved to the wall, near the window, was tugging at something. The bike. Merle was pulling at his bike.

Now he didn't care about the fire. He barely felt the heat. He slipped through the burning refuse to the old man. "Leave it, Merle!" he yelled. Merle's hair was on fire, his shirt reduced to a clinging black film. Blisters bubbled on the old man's arms and face.

"You're on fire!" A.J. yelled. He jerked savagely at Merle's arm.

The old man grunted as the bike came free from a burning timber section that had fallen from one of the roof joists. He turned, shoved the bike at A.J.

A.J.'s chest crackled as the hot metal ground into his flesh. He pushed Merle and the bike away, staggered toward the doorway. Part of the portal flexed, then fell in a snake of flames. A fireman caught A.J., dragged him to the drive, wrapped him in a blanket.

"Merle!" A.J. tried to point.

The fireman, a jowly man with short, gray hair, grimaced. "There's somebody else in there?"

He nodded. "Merle," he said again, weaker. A rainbow of water arched into the flames. Other firemen scurried about, yelling. An approaching EMC vehicle's siren, oscillating ever closer. Before he lost consciousness, he saw Merle stagger from the garage holding the bike, warped and blackened, an aura of smoke and flame about him.

A.J. woke in mid-afternoon in a hospital room. Bandages covered most of his chest and back and legs. He tried to get up, yelled at the pain.

A nurse entered, took his pulse, then secured a pair of bandages A.J. had inadvertently torn away from one arm.

"Where's Merle? Need to see Merle."

"Your guardian's in intensive care. He's unconscious."

"Need to see him."

The nurse gave him a tight-lipped smile. "I'm sorry, but you need rest."

He tried to get up again, yelped, slumped, and passed out.

Three days later, another nurse helped A.J. up and into a wheelchair. She turned him over to an orderly, who made cheerful small talk as he pushed A.J. toward ICU. They stopped before Merle's bed. "You can't have him but a couple of minutes," the orderly whispered as he pushed the chair forward.

A.J. pedaled closer, bent as much as his raw, cracked skin would allow. "Merle!"

The old man's head shook. His eyes opened.

"You with me, Merle?"

The old man blinked. "Tried save letters—"

"I know, Merle. I saw. But I didn't really want those."

"Bike."

"You caught fire when the chest of drawers went over. Why'd you want to save all that stuff?"

"Lost you. Jerry."

He wasn't sure what Merle meant, and he was angry the old man had risked his life that way. No, actually he was glad. Merle wasn't totally crazy. Even in his disturbed, drunken state, he'd made a gesture, risked death to save A.J.'s last treasured things.

"You're confused Merle. I'm not Jerry, if that's what you meant."

"Same," Merle mumbled.

The orderly returned, gently set a hand on A.J.'s shoulder. "You got to let him go now. He needs rest."

A.J. shoved the hand away. He realized Merle was appealing, in his oblique way, to their common lineage, to their blood, and something about that held A.J. captive. He wanted to resist, he had to. He'd already enlisted in the Navy, and he couldn't get out of it. But somehow he had to provide for the old man; he couldn't leave for the Navy before he was sure Merle would be cared for. A fist-sized lump rose in his throat. "When I get out of the hospital, I'll do something, maybe get you into a nursing home. Then I have to leave for boot camp. You understand, Merle?"

A nurse entered and stopped, hands clasped before her. "You really need to leave," she said. "He's very weak."

A.J. waved her away, anger rising again. "Damn it Merle, why'd you have to let yourself go like that?"

"Up in air," Merle mumbled.

"Up in the air? What's up in the air?"

"You. Me."

The nurse insisted now, her tone harsh. She motioned for the orderly to back A.J.'s wheelchair away.

"Not yet." A.J. commanded. "What the hell are you talking about, Merle? There's nothing up in the air. Do you understand I'm going away? It's settled. I have to."

"Nova Scotia. Fam'ly."

The old man was raving again. His lips moved again, but no words came.

The orderly turned the wheelchair, pushed A.J. toward the door.

"Sea," Merle croaked, loudly. "Sea."

A.J. held up a hand and the orderly stopped.

"You. Jong. Leur."

A.J. turned, burn pain searing him. The old man wants to keep me here, his prisoner. Maybe pain had addled A.J. too, but he was sure he could feel Merle's craziness creep over him, the way it had seemed to so many times before. He writhed to escape it.

"It's Royal, old man," he yelled back. "I'm not a Jongleur!"

But he knew that wasn't so. He had Jongleur blood, always would have, the same way he had Royal blood. Still, he had to distance himself from Merle and his disease, and from Weaverville and Asheville. He had to find the bright, illuminating life these insular mountains kept denying him. He had to make a place for Sandy and him in that world.

He and the orderly were in the hall now. A bell rang, kept ringing. Nurses raced toward Merle's room. A pair of doctors dashed by.

A.J. lurched, tried to look after them, but the orderly had turned the corner. Anyway, the pain was too much. His head dropped and his eyes closed. He knew what was going on in Merle's room. He began to sob. The orderly began a litany of soothing words.

I'm free now, A.J. thought, but he knew it wasn't so. Some onus he could feel but couldn't see had loosened its hold, but hadn't let go. Somewhere within him, a dark, sad emptiness yawned.

Katie and Art — 2002

Lord, Art Royal could aggravate. Take that fateful weekend a year ago, for example. He called late on Friday afternoon, somewhere the other side of Charlotte, where he'd been supervising a road project for Travelways Contracting, to tell me he'd picked up Mortie for the weekend. Gil Wayfarer, his assistant, was with him, too. Art had invited both to stay for dinner and an overnight. So there I was, cooking what I'd hoped would be a nice meal for the two of us, with leftovers for Saturday's lunch, and now I had to make dinner happen for four.

Mortie. Of all the aggravations Art ever caused me, he was the biggest. It all began one spring night a couple of years ago with a phone call. I'd been waiting on another agent to call about one of my property listings. I jumped up, but Art already had it. He was on a long while, part of it outside under the pretext of taking out the garbage, something he never did unless I nagged him. And trying to eavesdrop when he came back inside was a waste of time, because he mostly grunted and said Really? and That's great, and Uh huh. Finally he hung up and gave me a sheepish look, guilt written all over it.

I dropped the needlepoint to my lap, just knowing he was going to fib about something. He didn't do that often, but when he did, he'd squint a little and his face would turn red. It never failed. "Who was that?" I asked.

"You remember me telling you about that girl I dated senior year?"

Of course I remembered, how could I not? He used to go on and on about her, how good-looking she was, that cool convertible she had, how she was such a comfort during a difficult time. How old Merle, Art's great-grandpa, just adored her. As casually as I could, I said, "Sandy, wasn't it?"

"Right. Sandy."

His expression changed, then, telling me he was amazed I'd remember something as trivial as that. There wasn't a sign of a squint yet, but the blush was there.

"Well, that was her."

The needlepoint slipped off my lap. I glanced his way after picking it up and, lo and behold, there was the squint. "What'd she want?"

"Tracked me down, just wanted to connect, I guess, old school friends and such."

Uh huh. Guys might do that, but a woman doesn't cold call an old boyfriend just to say hello. There's always a reason. Be careful, Katie, I thought, don't let on you're upset, or you'll scare him. Let him dig himself in deeper. So I waited a second or two, then asked, "That's pretty odd, don't you think, calling out of the blue like that?"

He tossed the book he'd just picked up back on the coffee table, ran a hand through that mat of unruly dishwater blond hair, flipped on the TV and fell across his recliner, one of his long legs dangling over a chair arm.

"What'd she want?" I repeated.

He knew I hadn't bought that old friends business. You could almost see a big G for guilt on his forehead. The blush turned a bright crimson. All he could manage was, "Sandy?"

"Of course, Sandy. Your old flame. Your high school hottie."

He took a deep breath and smiled, probably figuring he'd charm his way back into my good graces.

I lost it then. I threw my needlepoint back on the floor and said, "Art Royal, turn off that TV and tell me what's going on. I mean it, right now!"

"Take it easy, Katie," he said. He hit the OFF button. "Just take it easy, okay?"

"I'll take it easy when you tell me what that phone call was about."

His voice took on a resigned tone, the kind somebody like him is left with when he's worked himself into a corner and the other person's going to regret asking. "Turns out she has a kid."

"A kid? Surely, you don't mean a billy goat."

He laughed, cleared his throat, and pushed himself to his feet. Hands in his pockets, he stood over me. Big people do that when they're trying to lord it over someone, especially small women such as myself.

"Right," he said. "A little boy. Mortie. Named him after her father. A goofy name for a kid these days, but he can always change it, I suppose."

"Okay," I said, giving him a cautious nod.

What was she looking for from Art? Probably in some sort of financial trouble, needed money. That's what happens to those intellectual, liberated, I Am Woman types. They rip off their bras and start trying to fight their way to the top of the men's world. When they can't make it, they run home to mama, an ex-husband, or some patsy like Art, who's still carrying a torch.

"All right, here it is," he said, edging onto the couch beside me and placing one big hand over both of mine, "She says Mortie's my son."

Well, he had me there. I was flabbergasted.

"We were very close back then. Intimate, I mean—"

"I know what intimate means," I said, hoping the moan I felt coming up wouldn't surface.

"She went to college at Chapel Hill, and I went into the Navy. We lost touch. If I'd known—"

The moan broke free. Lord help me, I thought, what am I going to do with this? I wanted to double up and bawl, but I couldn't; I had to get a handle on what this news meant, to me, to us.

He shifted closer, patted my hands. I pushed him away, my way of saying, This is no time for tenderness, Art Royal. "You would have married her," I said.

"Well, I don't know. I don't know what I would've done."

"You would've married her. That's what men do when they get carried away like that, acting on their urges. They have to pay for their sins."

"You know I don't think about it that way, Katie."

I pushed his hand away again. "Of course you don't. What am I thinking? You were raised a heathen. Then you left home, ran off to join the Navy, and left her holding the bag, didn't you? You had to go fight in that stupid Persian Gulf War. In the meantime, Sandy had to eke out a living. She had to raise little Mortie on her own."

He stood, backed away, fell across the recliner. "I don't think there's been much eking going on," he said. "Her family's well-off. They helped her, and after college she hustled up a job with a television station in Charlotte. A year later, they offered her a position as news anchor, and she took it. Now she heads the Governor's media team in Raleigh. Does consulting work on the side. All told, she knocks down in the low six figures."

"Then what does she want from you?"

"Like I said, just connecting." He smiled, squeezed my shoulder, picked up his book, and sat to read.

Despite my flying off the handle and his guilty looks, there didn't seem to be anything else to it. She thought Art should know he was a father, and after that, she never made any demands on us. In fact, this past fall she drove up, brought Mortie. She's rather nice, as it turns out, and much as I wanted her to, she just wouldn't give me a reason to dislike her. And she was gorgeous. Art said even more so than back then. Of course, he took to fatherhood, which was probably part of her master plan.

So here it was mid-January and Art was driving back from that construction job in Wilmington, had stopped in Raleigh to pick up Mortie for a long weekend, figuring I wouldn't mind. He'd asked Gil, too, to help with our addition, a loft over the garage for Mortie when he comes over.

And did I mention, among the other ghosts of Art's past, I had to endure living in the house he grew up in on South Main in Weaverville? He'd turned it into a real showpiece, I have to admit, painted inside in eggshell, my favorite. He even stained the kitchen cabinets in antique white and let me buy matching bedroom, living and dining furniture.

Art has a way with house building, with construction in general, something he picked up from that old Merle he had to live with. He told me some time back that after all the killing and burning in Kuwait and Iraq, he'd decided it was time to build things. He's always had a burr in his britches, though, and it wouldn't surprise me now to hear he's gone into land development. He talked a lot about it, even had an in with a big developer wanting to build out part of Elk Mountain. He promised me the listings if it worked out.

Anyway, he called twice more from the road, once while waiting for Gil to pick up some things in Hickory, then again deep in the mountains. Black ice was forming on the Interstate and he had to take it slow, so dinner went on the back burner. They finally drove up just after eight that evening.

"Katie!" he called out from the front door while Gil and Mortie stomped about on the front porch Art had added on. Knocking the slush off, I hoped.

I gave the corn a last stir to make sure it didn't scorch and called back, "Make sure they take those boots off." Having them scuffing my pretty hardwoods and tracking up the area rugs I'd just bought for the living and dining rooms was an absolute no-no, and Art knew it.

"We know the rules, ma'am," Gil laughed, and they came rumbling into the kitchen like the herd of heathens they are.

Art swept me up, gave me a kiss, beer on his breath. No wonder they were so jolly. Then he poked under the pot lids. Gil smiled, all sinewy and tall and good looking as can be, and he and Mortie backed up to the stove to warm their behinds.

Mortie was a handsome fella of twelve then, almost thirteen, and growing like a weed. He'll probably be taller than Art by the time he's done. He has his mother's brown hair and her eternally tanned look, and is in no way shy. He's going to drive the little girls wild. Their parents, I should say. After a good warming and a glance at his wristwatch, Mortie grinned and edged toward the living room. "I gotta watch the news. Mom's gonna be on."

Oh, that's just fine, I said to myself. A house full of guys wanting to watch TV, to see Mortie's mom, no less. So, as usual, I have to be the meanie. "No, honey, the news shows are long since over. Besides, dinner's ready."

"They're doing a profile on CNN," said Art. "It's just a two minute spot."

I turned off the burners and gave everything a last look while they trooped into the living room. The spot had just started, the sort of filler that's so popular these days, about beautiful, successful, husbandless mothers.

Oh, my. No wonder she landed that anchor job and now fronts for the Governor. She was made for the camera, even more beautiful under those glaring lights than in person. She managed to show off her cleavage without looking like a hussy, bestowed a winner of a smile on us you know she'd rehearsed, even gave her long hair a little flip as they panned away.

I glanced down. By comparison, my breasts looked like BBs inside this peanut shell-size bra of mine. And this stringy hair I've never been able to do anything with? It couldn't possibly hold up to that sort of exposure. I had to wonder what Art saw in me in the first place. After all, he and this beauty had had a child together and were now in constant touch. So maybe I'd been a substitute all the while, a skinny, string-haired convenience he was now ready to dump.

Well, they started clapping and yelling, and it was obvious Mortie was very proud of his mama. But what took me aback as we settled around the dinner table was the way Art kept beaming, as if proud of her for having birthed him such a fine son.

Fortunately, my dinner held up, with enough left over for seconds. They started bellowing for dessert, so I took an angel food cake from the freezer, microwaved it, and we had French vanilla with our slices. After that, we sat around the table and made after-dinner chitchat.

It wasn't too long before Mortie started playing his version of twenty questions with Art. He grilled him about his promotion to project superintendent with Travelways, and then Art grinned and went off on a tangent. It seems his daddy, Casey, once threw knives at some big doll. Art always gives you the details, and he made a big deal of how the knives glittered as they turned, blade over handle, point thunking into a tree, the shaft quivering as it stuck beside the doll's ear. Mortie oohed and wowed, and then Gil, who apparently knew more about the story than I did, changed the subject to Art's time in the Navy.

"Oh, yeah," said Mortie, "Mom said you were a war hero."

Art poked at the last of his ice cream, the grin gone. "Not hardly."

"He did bring home some medals," I said, trying to shore Art up.

"They give medals just for showing up," he mumbled.

"But that war was in the desert," Mortie said. "You can't be in the Navy and win medals in the desert."

Knowing Art's reluctance on the subject—it took me a full year to get anything out of him about it—I interrupted. "It's late, and you fellows are bushed. Why don't y'all get on to bed?"

"It's okay," Art said. "He should know about it."

So he started telling Mortie the story I'd heard, about his training after boot camp, graduating a gunner's mate. Boot camp gave him an awful itch to serve, like the old guy Merle had done, and he even thought about applying for training as a SEAL, but decided against it after hearing about the high dropout rate.

His first sea duty was to be on some sort of escort vessel, a frigate he called it, but a mine in the Middle East blew it up a month before he was to report. About that time, the Navy was calling for volunteers to serve on an oiler that had been commissioned the year before. That's a ship that keeps others supplied with fuel. He was so eager to get to sea he stepped forward.

So there he was, at sea for the first time. I remember his face lighting up every time he talked about the ocean. It was just the way he'd pictured it, he'd say, all wind and water, the ship chugging along as powerful as you can imagine. And before you know it, he was in the Middle East.

I swear, his testosterone must have built up until it dribbled out his ears. He told his officer he wanted duty closer to the action, but the war wound down without the transfer he wanted. He kept on pestering, though, going on and on about how a gunner's mate was a waste on an oiler. Finally the officer gave in and had orders cut transferring him to a destroyer coming out of the shipyards a few months later.

While the ship underwent testing, Art passed his time playing Navy baseball. It'd been some time since he'd played, but he was a natural at it and developed a pretty good reputation as a relief pitcher. He even had an offer to take a plum job near Washington so he could play regularly. But no, Art Royal had to go to sea on that new destroyer.

And that's how he ended up on the commissioning crew of the USS *Fitzgerald* late in 1995, I think it was, taking part in that silly thing where they run on board to bring the ship to life. Then there was a little more training in missiles aboard a floating school, his job to shoot something called Tomahawks at whatever enemies raised their ugly heads.

A few months passed and right before his second enlistment ended, off he went, back to the Middle East on another ship, the *Hewitt*. Saddam had just booted some U.S. inspectors out of the country. Pretty soon the *Hewitt* was sitting over there primed to get its licks in, Art as eager as any to get into the thick of it.

At this point in the story, Mortie was twisting in his chair, eyes wide as saucers. "Did you take some of them out, Dad?" You could tell he had Art's blood running in him, and I got the feeling he'd do pretty much the same thing as his daddy, given the chance.

Art set his napkin on the table and frowned. He glanced my way, then to Mortie. "There's one thing you and I have to get straight right now, young man. It's an ugly business. Not the least bit glamorous, you understand?"

Mortie blinked, swallowing hard at being chastised out of the blue like that. "Yessir," he mumbled. That was the first I'd seen of proper manners from the boy. As much as I hated the idea, maybe Art was good for him.

Gil chuckled, a grin spreading across his handsome face. "Come on, Art, answer the kid's question."

Art found something on the tabletop to stare at and didn't answer for a minute. I'd come to realize this was Art sifting through his emotions, looking for the right words. Finally eyes narrowed, he set his jaw. As it turned out, it was something I was about to hear for the first time.

"Yeah," he said in a low growl, "I did take some of them out. The skipper ordered us to fire a Tomahawk, then another."

"But you couldn't see the damage," Gil prompted.

Now Art was pulling at a shirt button, and for a second I thought he'd wrench it off. He continued in a voice I'd never heard before, something from his past, I imagine, a singsong sort of talk in an odd accent.

"I saw it, now," he said, "I saw it just fine. My buddy Jake was working in CIC, that's the Combat Information Center, and he showed me films. They put cameras on those birds. They can hover them over the target, drop bomblets, and then take pictures."

"Wow!" said Mortie.

Gil shook his head, clearly caught up in this. "That's real sci-fi stuff. I had no idea."

Art stood and started pacing. His regular voice returned, but it was shaky, awfully shaky. "It started for me when we touched off the first Tomahawk. The missile cell glowed, fire came out of it, and then the ship shook a little. Off it went, like a giant Roman candle."

He kicked at my new platinum area rug, like something was on it no one could see but him.

"Boom!" said Mortie.

Art leveled a finger at him. "Don't." Then he took a deep breath and collected himself.

Mortie slumped into his chair, pouting. I just can't imagine that boy'd ever been corrected twice in a row like that, especially by a man, and over such a little thing.

"You know, I might've seen some of that on the news," said Gil. "I swear, you'd never see explosions like that during demolition."

"It was like that, all right," said Art, staring a hole in the rug. "Lit up Baghdad like you wouldn't imagine."

My antenna always started twitching when this sort of mood hit Art. You see, I'd been concerned for some time about my feelings for him, Sandy and Mortie only making it worse. Something would set him off, and he'd crawl into that shell of his, not saying ten words in a day. I was starting to get the feeling we were living alone in the same house, but by now I knew it wasn't my fault. Something about this part of the story, his jumping on Mortie, made me realize there was this big hole in Art, a void I knew nothing about, maybe something he wasn't even in touch with. So I made him back up a minute to get at it. "What started?"

He stared at me, not understanding.

"You said something started when you shot the first Tomahawk."

He scuffed the rug again. "It was Merle. He started talking to me."

We all hushed. I don't know about the others, but I had no idea how to take this.

"He started saying things to me." Art eyed Gil, then Mortie, then me. Looking down, he said, "Doesn't make a lot of sense, does it?"

"Go on with it," I said, wanting him to get it out. Maybe this would clear his decks, as he was so fond of saying. Maybe the thing in him would surface, and then he and I could make our way through the space that had grown between us. "What was it Merle was saying?"

He swallowed, eyes flitting back and forth like a crazy person. "You see, A.J.?" he began in that odd singsong. "You just beginning to get a dose of what I had to deal with over there in France. You're gonna have to pay attention to the water, Sonny. Pay attention to the water."

Then he tore into the story of old Merle's LST landing in France, words coming like they were shooting out under pressure. He wound that one down and finished the Tomahawk story by saying, "I wasn't responding to the Missile Officer fast enough, could hardly pay attention at all. He got so upset he relieved me."

Gil wrenched himself from his chair. It was as if Art had spread some contagious thing, and Gil was afraid he'd catch it. "Who the hell's A.J.?"

"Him," I answered. "A.J. is Art. That's what he used to be called."

"Hard to make sense of all that now," said Art. "Merle used to come apart when I was a kid. He'd start mumbling, acting crazy. After awhile, I understood he was hallucinating about World War II, the stuff he went through. I'd watch it rise in him, like a fever, and then it'd slip across the room, come after me. A couple years of that, and I had to get away from the old guy."

"It sounds to me like you were identifying with his war experiences," said Gil. "Which makes me wonder why you wanted to go to war yourself."

"I don't suppose I'd ever thought it through," Art said. "Afraid to, I guess. I wanted to serve, come home, be proud of it. But now I'm afraid I'll end up like Merle, and Casey. Crazy as a bedbug."

"You won't, honey," I said, "you didn't even see any fighting. And you aren't like you said your daddy Casey was."

He glanced my way. His face was hardly recognizable, it was so twisted with anguish. "I have his blood," he said. "I felt what he felt, and what happened to him could still happen to me."

Mortie wriggled in his chair, saying nothing. One hand tugged on the other, like they were stuck together. Then all of a sudden he jumped up and ran down the hall and ducked into the bathroom.

"I can see how you could think that, I guess," Gil said.

At this point, I had to get in my two cents worth. "Well, not me," I declared. Things were getting too gloomy, and what he was saying wasn't close to being believable. The way he was going on, it was more like those weird European movies he got interested in after being in the Navy. I wanted him to get past that low mood. And I wanted to understand how it was for him deep down inside, without his dressing it up in fairy tales.

"I realize Merle wormed his way into you with that craziness of his," I said, "and I suppose that can poison a person's mind. But how could you let it get to you in the middle of shooting those Tomahawks? And hearing Merle talking, well, I don't believe that, not for a second."

"Don't be too sure," said Gil. "I've seen things like that happen on the job site. It's herd instinct, or something. Somebody'll slip and fall, and the others start thinking about it. They pass it on by facial expressions is my theory, maybe by the way they carry themselves. Or maybe it's a little like the way birds fly in a flock when they're migrating. From a distance, they act like one big bird, with one in the lead."

I was about to say I couldn't see that either when Art drew his lips into a line, stuck his chin out, and said, "It was stronger than that. Merle was so real you could almost reach out and touch him."

"I don't follow," Gil said.

We sat waiting for Art to say something more. Finally, he said, "When you're little, the way the grownups around you live determines the way you see the world. Then when you're an adult, maybe you have a different take on it. But try as you might, you can't get away from the way you saw the world as a child. Merle was a part of my childhood and, well, all he went through, I don't think those things are going to be settled as long as I'm around."

Mortie had returned from the bathroom, as antsy as can be. "Can I go to bed now?"

Relieved to have an opening in this crazy talk, I got up. "It is almost midnight, and we do need to get up early.

Art, you get Mortie situated and I'll make up the couch for Gil."

I thought that would break the mood, but it didn't. It took over an hour for Art to get Mortie calmed down. I cleaned up the kitchen, Gil settling into the living room, where I couldn't help but watch him, as big and strong as Art, maybe even more so. An ominous feeling had settled in, not at all what I wanted with company in the house, and I guess I kept watching Gil to get my mind straight.

Later, Art busied himself in the bedroom with first one thing then another, and I fell asleep. When I woke to use the bathroom a couple of hours later, I noticed him on his back, wide awake.

I slipped back under the covers and put a leg over his, my hand on his bare chest, over the burn marks from a time when Merle burned their garage. "You still in a mood?"

"It's not a mood," he growled as he pushed me away. "The stuff with Merle, it's real."

"No, it's not real, it's an obsession."

He let out a sigh, moonlight from the bedroom window putting shadows on him and making his frown ever so ugly.

So I climbed out of bed again, pulled the curtains together, crawled back under the covers, and kissed him. "It'll be better in the morning," I whispered.

Most of the time with these moods, he'd toss and turn until daylight, but now he fell fast asleep. Lying there thinking, I remembered his telling me he wanted out after firing those missiles at Saddam, even got crawled when his

Executive Officer saw the request to leave the Navy early. That officer, an Academy graduate and gung-ho type, threatened, then sweet-talked, and eventually they sat down and talked it out.

"This was nothing," the officer told him. "We're just a missile delivery system, shooting at a world-class bad guy who can hardly shoot back. What if he'd had ships? What if he'd fired missiles at us, out here in coastal waters? We'd be taking hits, people getting killed, your buddies and mine. Hell, Royal, you volunteered for this. You shouldn't be getting so upset over a few missile shots."

Art said the officer was right; it really shouldn't have upset him, because he'd been trained for exactly that. But he *was* upset, and he just couldn't get past it. "I don't know, sir," he told the officer, "I honestly don't know what happened. Maybe I heard too much about this sort of thing when I was a kid." He told the lieutenant commander his grandpa had died in Vietnam, then about old Merle dying a slow, crazy death over a string of years. "I'm sorry, but I can't deal with it," he told the man, "that's all I know." Finally, the officer gave up, and Art flew home before the ship's deployment ended. He'd just signed on for another four years, so he finished up at a desk job in Norfolk, Virginia.

During that time, a coach who knew about his pitching picked him up as a relief pitcher for the Navy–Marine Corps baseball game. He didn't play, he said, but it was fun to suit up one last time. And he did manage to leave the Navy early, because of all the leave time he'd built up.

Just before falling asleep, sometime after two in the morning, I remembered a piece he used to recite when he was in a mood and I'd ask him what the matter was. The piece was a reflection of sorts, written by some old poet he liked. He had me memorize it so we could say it together, like a Bible verse. It got to be a joke between us, but the words grew on me:

> "Man consists of more pieces, more parts, than the world; than the world doth, nay than the world is. And if these pieces were extended and stretched out in man as they are in the world, man would be the giant and the world the dwarf, the world but the map, and the man the world."

It sounded Biblical to me, the Bible being something Art just wouldn't take any comfort in. Heaven knows, I tried every way I could to get him to make his peace with the Lord, but he said with all he'd seen and heard, it didn't help. So maybe each of us has to get our comfort wherever we can, even from dead poets and the like.

It was after ten that morning when sunlight peeking around the bedroom curtains woke me. There wasn't any hammering, and no men's heavy steps. Gil had come to help Art sheetrock the loft, and there should've been some sort of noise. I looked down on South Main Street and noticed Art's truck gone. Maybe they needed some more nails or sheetrock. Or maybe they hadn't wanted to wake me and were eating at the Waffle House.

Downstairs, a dirty skillet and dishes had been dumped in the sink, jam and crumbs and orange juice and coffee spills all over the kitchen table. I poured the rest of the coffee for myself, cut a bagel, dropped both pieces in the toaster, and cinched up my robe against the cold to pick up the morning paper. A light snow had fallen during the night. The sun on it was almost blinding. A brisk wind was rolling on down the street. Back inside, I took my eats and coffee and paper to the living room, and decided to make it a lazy morning.

Noon came, and still no Art and Gil and Mortie. I read the paper, tidied the kitchen, and after putting clothes in the wash, I pulled out a magazine I'd picked up at the grocery store. Then guilt began to set in. Guilt, I think, at being happy to have so much weekend time to myself.

I hate to admit it, but Art was my first long-term relationship. Oh, I'd dated regularly, even had my share of Saturday night sleepovers, but nothing lasting. After giving up secretarial work, I took a real estate course, passed the tests, moved out of Mama's place over in Leicester, rented an apartment of my own off Tunnel Road, and started selling. I was pretty good at it, too, especially the finance part. There were some long days and weeks getting established, and I lived and breathed it with not much time to spare for things such as romance. Seven, maybe eight years went by, and what happens? I meet Art.

I'd been checking my listings at the office, and his knock startled me. He smiled. Immediately, those good looks had me going, especially the ice-blue eyes. He was all keyed up. He bounced on his toes and told me the Fates were at work; the house he'd grown up in was for sale. He'd just taken a job with a construction company and only had five thousand dollars from his Navy pay to spare. He wanted to know if that would be enough for a down payment.

The house wasn't familiar for some reason, so I looked it up in the multi-list and discovered it was a fixer-upper, asking price just under a hundred thousand, the owner open to offers. So we piled into my Cherokee and drove over.

It looked even worse than the description. It had that awful asbestos siding, and its shingles were all curled up. The attic showed signs of leaks, and the living spaces were a filthy, mildewed, smelly mess. "I'm sorry," I said. "I wouldn't have thought it'd be this bad."

He put a hand on my arm and smiled. "Not a problem. I can fix it up."

I have to admit I liked him being so close I could smell his aftershave. Oh, who am I kidding? It excited me to no end. Struggling to keep my wits about me, I considered the price and his hopeful down payment. "At this price," I had to tell him, "I'm not sure five thousand will be enough for a V.A. loan."

He just smiled again and asked, "Can we make an offer?"

The owner, a Mr. Bretherton, turned out to be an acquaintance of my broker's, and he was available so, standing in that nasty living room, I made the offer over my cell phone.

"Fifty thousand?" Mr. Bretherton chuckled. "Who is this guy?"

"A former sailor, and he's handy," I told him. "He says he can fix it up himself."

"Put him on the phone, will you, Katie?"

He and Art had a long talk about the Navy, Mr. Bretherton having been a tin can sailor, whatever that is, just after the Korean War. After some haggling, they settled on sixty-five thousand.

"We should celebrate," Art said after he'd signed the offer. "How about dinner?"

It seemed the Lord's own work. One thing led to another, very quickly, I might add, and we took up living in my place while Art worked on his new house. In the meantime, he enrolled in tech school at night here in Asheville and finished a year later. When he had the house just perfect, we had another celebration: a small church wedding and five glorious days honeymooning in Cozumel.

So what was at the root of my guilt at enjoying quiet time alone in that very house? I suppose it was being thirty-six and still not used to living with someone else. Maybe I'm the hermit type, work having always been there to keep the loneliness off me. Flipping through the magazine, thoughts kept coming up. Are you happy with Art? Is this marriage working? If you leave will it be better? Would you miss him terribly? Would you like living alone again? Would you ever want to remarry? At that point and in quite an emotional sweat, I heard Art's truck doors slam, then voices.

"Katie!" he called out. "You have to see this!"

Mortie burst in, as worked up as I'd ever seen a boy. "He got me a bike!" he yelled. "It's a classic!"

"Shh," I cautioned as I got up, not yet back from my worries, a hand out to keep him and his muddy boots off my nice floor. "A bike?"

Mortie pulled me out the door, still in my robe. Now I was wishing I'd at least taken the time to brush my hair and put on a touch of makeup. A bright sun like that can make you look years older, even to your husband.

Art lowered his truck's tailgate and lifted out a bike. It had high handlebars and some sort of stick thing attached to a bar in front of the seat, which was a long, saddle-shaped affair.

Seeing that, I had to ask myself what Art was getting us into, buying this boy a bike. He has a well-off mother, and even if you forgot she's a former flame of Art's, you had to figure if we kept doing things like this for him, they'd both start expecting it.

Despite the cold, Art had taken off his coat, sleeves rolled up, showing that little hummingbird tattoo he got on his forearm somewhere in the Mediterranean. He lifted the bike to his shoulder, pressed the tires, ran a finger over the brand new chain, then bounced the bike on the sidewalk.

"It's my old one," he said, eyes gleaming. "Mortie's mom kept it for me all those years I was in the Navy. That was part of why she called, to see if I still wanted it."

Hmm. He'd never said a word about a bike. Or going to her house to get it.

"It was a mess," Gil added. "It had been through a fire, and the metal was warped to beat the band. We did some straightening at the company shop. Art's been working on it ever since."

Art squinted, his face shining like a little boy's on Christmas morning. "All except the handlebars and pedal assembly. Had a pro re-chrome those for me." He ran a hand over the handlebars, then every inch of the newly painted frame and wheel guards. The paint looked white at first, but maybe that was glare from the snow. After a closer look, I realized he'd painted it pale blue, just enough tint in a white base to have the blue show.

"It was Marie's originally," he told me. "It was red when she got it, something called an Apple Krate, a boy's bike, but a really neat one for a kid back then."

"I wanted him to restore it the way it had been," said Gil. "The serial number plate's still attached, and if it'd been restored, it'd be worth maybe a couple thousand to a collector."

Art had allowed a weird expression, some extreme look of happiness, wild and serene at the same time. I'd seen glimmers of it before, even the day I met him. Maybe that's part of what drew me to him and out of the pat little life I'd been living. Noticing me staring, he let it go, a smug smile taking its place.

"Didn't want to restore it," he said. "This way we wouldn't be tempted to sell it. It was blue when I had it, and didn't want to see that dark, ugly shade again. Wanted

Carolina blue, but a couple shades lighter, something elegant." He turned to Mortie. "Want to take it out for a spin?"

"Art," I said, "the walk's still frozen. He'll slip and fall."

"It's okay," Mortie said, "I'm good at riding."

Art held the bike while Mortie climbed on, gave him a shove, and watched him pedal, the first few yards on the ice unsteady as can be. Then he picked up speed and started pedaling like a veteran.

"Get in the street, go that way a few houses," Art yelled, taking a couple of steps uphill. "Then you can ride it down to the school."

Gil and I watched them awhile before I turned to the door. "I'll make y'all some sandwiches," I called back, "but I need a shower first."

As I showered, I could hear Gil driving nails out in the garage loft. For some reason, I kept picturing him in the shower with me, felt his hands washing my back, then my breasts, giving me those tingles I used to get from Art. While drying my hair, I caught a man scent, and it wasn't Art's. I found a pair of corduroy pants I hadn't put on in a year, a bit too snug now, and pulled them on. Turning before the bathroom mirror, I realized my figure was nothing to sneeze at. Then I added a fluffy off-white sweater, which was a bit tight now, too, one that always went well with this red hair of mine.

I called to Mortie and Art that sandwiches would be ready in fifteen minutes. Mortie wanted soup. Gil finished what he was doing, so he sat at the kitchen table while I opened a couple of cans, mixed them, and began a simmer. We chatted, and during the sandwich making he joked about Art's working on the bike, and then we talked about the work in the loft. I had to tend to lunch, but I could feel his eyes on me the whole time.

After we'd eaten, Art began wondering out loud whether he ought to keep the bike at the house or carry it back to Raleigh when he took Mortie home.

"He'll get to use it more if he takes it with him," I said, not knowing whether I was looking out for Mortie's interests or mine.

"Yeah," said Mortie.

Art laughed. "All right, it's settled. The bike goes to Raleigh."

Gil pushed his plate away. "Guess I'll do a little more with the sheetrock." He smiled. "You guys come along when you get your feet back on the ground."

"Ah," said Art. "I'm out of the sheetrock mood. Son, you want to ride some more?"

"Yeah, down to the school again," the boy said. "The bike's radical, Dad."

Art handed him his coat, put an arm over his shoulder, and off they went.

I tidied the kitchen and settled in with my magazine, but Mortie's yelps kept tugging at me. So I pulled on a jacket and some mittens and watched them from the porch. It had warmed a little and the ice on the walkway was melting. Art was laughing and Mortie whooping. A few minutes later, the hammering upstairs stopped. Gil joined me.

"There's too much excitement out here," he said, leaning over the rail next to me.

I tried to ignore the smell of him, imagined his warmth, a figment in the cold air. Lord in heaven, what are you trying to tell me? I thought. I'm bored with Art, and now have the hots for Mister Gil Wayfarer? Please don't let that happen. I don't know if I can live with the upshot. So I snuggled into my jacket and watched Art and Mortie up the hill.

They were talking, Art pointing, making swooping motions with his hands and Mortie nodding. Then they laughed and Mortie climbed off the bike.

"You know," said Gil, "I'm not the world's best judge of women, but it seems to me something's on your mind."

I gave him a look and said nothing. Up the street, Art was straddling the bike.

But Gil kept on. "What's the matter?" he said. "Art can't scratch your itch any more?"

That time I frowned. "Gil, you're being awfully forward."

He laughed, then stared at his boots. "Yeah, guess I am at that."

Water was rattling through the downspouts from the snowmelt from the roof. It cut a trough through a strip of yard snow and dribbled down to the end of the drive, where it disappeared, along with another half-dozen streams, into the gutter. That made me feel a little warmer somehow. We both watched Art bend over the bike, then pedal like mad, all elbows and knees. He picked up speed, such a happy look on his face as he passed the house. A little boy in a big, strong body.

Gil had moved closer, one of his hands touching mine. "But I'm betting you don't mind my being a little forward." The gleam in his eye and the devilish grin could just as well have been Art's. I let his hand cover mine.

All of a sudden I blurted, "You know I'm thinking about leaving him."

The hand slipped away. He pulled a pack of cigarettes from his jacket pocket and lit one. "Really."

Why did I have to say that? Lord, are you guiding me here? Is this what you want? Do you want me to take up with my husband's best friend, like some trailer trash mama? "But I haven't come to a decision on anything," I added. "I might stay, who knows? It's just that—"

"The kid," he interrupted. "The kid's a problem. And his mom's getting to you because of her history with Art."

Art had turned around in the school parking lot and was fiddling with the stickshift thing. I lifted the cigarette from Gil's hand and drew on it. Now why did I do that? I don't smoke anymore. It just seemed, you know, the thing to do, like in the movies when some vamp is trying to decide which naughty thing she's going to pull next. "Art and I have tried and tried to have a child."

"He told me."

"It just won't happen. I never wanted anything more than to cement this marriage, make it work, live a normal, Godly life together."

He took the cigarette back and, well, I almost started crying. Now stop it, Katie Evans, I thought—Katie Royal, I mean—you have a good life, and here you go, wanting to spoil it. Then I felt Art's—no, Gil's—arm around my shoulder, his strength drawing me to him.

"Are you okay?"

I pulled free, turned away, and wiped my eyes with a sleeve before I faced him again. "Do you want to have an affair?"

Looking stunned, he edged away, stubbed out his cigarette on the porch rail, eyed me up and down. I might as well have been standing there naked on that cold January afternoon.

"You and me?"

"Yes," I said, "do you see anybody else out here?"

He gave me that devilish grin again. "Now why in the world would you come up with that?"

Oh, Lord. You've really put your foot in your mouth this time, Katie. I'd had him figured as the type to jump at a proposition like that, and then he starts playing games. "Forget it, Gil. Just forget it."

"No, no, I just thought you and Art might have had some kind of talk, that's all." He backed away a step, let out a careful sigh. "I sure don't want to be the one to pull you off the marriage merry-go-round," he said, emphasis on I.

"Talk?" Was Art planning to leave me? Suddenly I felt a little faint. "What kind of talk?"

"I don't know. Like you said, Katie, forget it."

Art waved to Mortie, set the stickshift, and pedaled uphill. There was that little boy look again, like he was happy to be out of school, hurrying home to his mama. Bent low, knees making those awkward loops in the air as he pedaled, he passed us, Mortie cheering him on.

Then it dawned on me why Gil was dancing around what I'd said. It was the commitment thing. He had the idea I was thinking marriage, that I'd sink my hooks into him the way I had Art. And what was I thinking, anyway, offering to add a risky relationship to the iffy one I already had. So, figuring I could cover my tracks a little with some teasing, I said, "What is it with you men? You want your cake, but you're not the least bit interested in buying it. Not that that was what I had in mind, anyway."

He laughed and seemed relieved, bent over the rail to watch Mortie take the bike. Then he gave me a cocky look, kind of like the one Art has at times, but a bit more wicked. "Look at you, Katie, you're up in the air over this Mortie thing, so you're out shopping. Is that any better than me wanting to make love to you without any complications?"

I had to laugh. Subtle as a train wreck, that, even after my come-on. "Gil Wayfarer," I replied, "you sure know how to sweet-talk a girl."

His grin widened. "Well, let me know."

Let him know my rear end. Like he said, I was up in the air over Mortie, maybe the marriage too, and I was looking for an out. I just hoped he wouldn't say something to Art.

Now Mortie was pushing the bike back home, Art walked behind him, flushed and happy. Nearing the house, they could have been the same person, one a miniature of the other, Mortie's looks so much like his daddy's. Art was still excited and kid-like. It was as clear as the nose on your face that this was good for him. Something he'd needed for a long, long time, and I realized I'd been selfish to begrudge him time with his own son.

"Runs like a Swiss watch," said Art. "Man, oh, man, I wish it'd been like this when I had it."

Gil joined in, slapping backs, admiring the bike with them. "Mortie," he teased, "I think you just lost your bike."

Art and the boy tugged the bike back and forth, faking angry faces. Then Mortie reached up and hugged his daddy's neck. Art held him for a long while, my stomach sinking into the vacant place where our own child would never be.

"Snow's coming back tonight," said Gil. "If we're going back east, we'd better hop to it."

Art turned to me, his expression begging.

Okay, I nodded, one more night wouldn't hurt. "You'll do no such thing," I said, "I'll fix supper and you're all spending the night here."

Mortie pumped a fist. "All right!" He dashed in the house to call his mom, muddy boots and all.

"Nope," said Art. "You aren't fixing dinner. I'm taking everyone to downtown Weaverville for pizza."

I went in to fix my face and brush the frizzes out of my hair. Gil helped them clean up the bike. Ten minutes later, it sat on the front porch, gleaming again. We backed away to admire it, a testament to, I don't know, the sometimes awful connections we make and can never shake. The bike's faint blue in the deep, perfect paint came to the fore as the sun began to fall, as if it were waking up, kind of like those mood rings girls used to wear. Then something in the sun reflected in it, a wild, leaping flame of some sort, there for an instant and gone.

After our pizza supper, Art and Gil had a few more beers apiece than I thought they should. I made Gil's bed on the sofa. Mortie fell asleep the minute he closed his eyes.

Maybe it was the beer, but Art was glowing. He kept chattering as we got ready for bed. "Didn't that bike turn out great? I wasn't sure I could get the paint color right, so I just kept spraying and buffing, made it as deep as I could, and finally it turned out. And the stickshift, I wish it had worked that well for me. Gil, he helped me calibrate it. Man, that thing will really go."

He was sitting on the edge of the bed in his underwear. Already in bed and tired of hearing about it, I rolled over, put a hand over his mouth, whispered, "Shh." He laughed, reached back to tug at my T-shirt, and pulled me to him.

Then he leaned his head into my chest, his way of begging me to run a hand over his face, talk babytalk to him, the way a mother would. He always did bring the mother out in me, and that night I found it, oh, so easy to play that part. Finally, he lay back and clawed the T-shirt off me.

On that cold night, as we made love, something happened. I opened up to him in a way I never had before. It was like I was consumed by a fire we both shared. I closed my eyes, everything spinning, me tumbling through space, going places I'd never imagined existed.

I could only guess how it affected Art, though. I tried to talk with him about it before we fell asleep, but all he'd do was grunt. He finally said something about thinking he'd never have that feeling again.

"Sure we can, Art. We just did, and we can again. We can keep on having it."

He turned, and in the dark I could barely make out his expression, one I couldn't decipher, like he was in a place far away and didn't know how to escape from it. He rolled over and fell fast asleep.

Then it hit me. He hadn't meant he'd never have that feeling again with me. It was Sandy. He'd had it with her, and he'd thought he'd never have it with anyone else. So that was it. I'd finally figured out what made Mister Art Royal tick. He was never going to allow himself to break free from the hold she had on him.

Come on, Katie, I told myself, are you really jealous of a high school girlfriend? Are you really unhappy enough to make something out of Art battling with his past?

But was it such a little a thing? I mean, it seemed small enough after the fantastic sex we'd just had, but how much of a gulf was there between us because of what Art did when he wasn't even eighteen years old? And how much did the Navy and his mama and daddy and Merle affect us? Okay, I did consider having an affair with Gil, so I had to ask myself, whose gulf was it? Art's or mine?

Well, forget Gil. You've been thinking about leaving Art anyway, Katie. No, something else's eating at you. It was there before this Sandy and Mortie thing, so what's wrong?

That took me back to the day Art and I met and that first year. I was feeling a little lonely and hadn't realized it back then, and there he was, this handsome ex-sailor, ready and willing to sweep me off my feet. We didn't really get to know each other, just started living together, then got married, all of it built around his fantasy of living in that house.

That was it—he was living a dream, or maybe a nightmare. Had been for years, still trying to escape from that nasty old Merle he lived with. Art dreaming about Sandy all the while. And buying the house reminded him of Marie, his mama. Then there was his daddy, Casey, who'd gone nuts and was still in and out of jail.

There'd never be room for me in a world so crowded with people from his past, especially Marie, but most especially Sandy. That was why I wanted to leave, why I had to leave.

Sleep came then, the thrashing sort that gives you no peace at all. Just as the sky started lightening he turned over, an arm across my breasts. On impulse I pressed his hand, made him squeeze me, and he woke. Without another word we made love again. And again it was the same way, all crackles and sparks, like a fireworks show between us. Lord in heaven, I'd never imagined anything like that before. I was so swept up in it, just going with it, not caring where it took me.

Afterward, we didn't talk about it. He curled up like a little boy, and I took him in. I'd never have a child of my own, knowing it moving inside me, feeding off me, kicking, feeling its heartbeat against mine. But holding Art that way was enough for now. I was his Marie that morning. Maybe that sounds wicked and unChristian, but I didn't care. It was enough, that's all I know. It was enough.

We fixed breakfast together, the day promising to be another bright one, but almost a gale blowing down South Main, three inches of fresh snow on the ground. No one wanted to leave the warm kitchen, but Art finally got them moving, and they loaded their bags and the bike into his truck.

He started the engine while Gil scraped the windshield. Mortie kept peering though the truck's rear window at the bike. Then Art dashed up the walk, met me at the threshold, wrapped me in those long arms, and we kissed.

Laughing, he let go.

"What?"

"The bike. It's going to blow Sandy's mind," he whispered.

Ever so slowly I pushed him away.

He looked at me like I'd never understand anything. "It was an old piece of junk when she last saw it," he said. "I used to imagine she thought of me the same way, you know? Some piece of trash she went slumming with for a year before moving back into her whitebread world."

He threw a glance Mortie's way, then back to me. "Look, Mortie doesn't have to be a problem between us. Sandy's doing fine, spends a lot of time with him, doesn't want child support. I can see him every now and then and leave it at that."

This was what I'd been waiting to hear from him. I should have thrown my arms around him, maybe cried a little, but I didn't. Instead I backed away another step, hugged my shoulders. "Nonsense, Art, he's your son. You want him to be all screwed up, think his daddy's abandoned him? After all those years of hearing about you, and then having weekends like this, and a new bike his daddy built?"

As I said that, his shoulders dropped in relief. "You're such a champ," he said. "I love you so much."

"I love you," I replied, a little weaker than I should have.

He leaped the porch steps, a quick look to the sky, rounded his truck, slid in, and they were off, waving. He tooted the horn as they made a U turn. I waved back and ducked inside.

Mortie's sheets and ours were in the wash, then I remembered Gil's. Before dropping them in, I sniffed. I wanted to remember his scent, the way I'd always enjoyed smelling Art on our sheets, on me. I pressed them into the washer, water and agitator pulling the sheets down, taking their smells away. Afterward, I spent a long while getting the kitchen spic and span, straightened up the living room and, after a shower, cleaned the bathroom from top to bottom.

There. Now yesterday's gone, Art's gone, and Gil and Mortie are gone. I'm here by myself, at last, and will be all day. This is what I wanted, isn't it? I turned on the TV, then switched it off. Silence. There weren't any distractions now, any complications, just me, in this nice, warm, white house.

I had to think about it. I had the time and the opportunity, so I needed to get over my wishy-washy feelings and decide: Should I stay with Art?

I lay back on the couch, eyes closed, for maybe an hour. I got up and put the sheets in the dryer. Then I walked down the street, thought about Gil and Art, about Mortie and his mama. Still, nothing came to me in the way of a decision.

Then all of a sudden I knew. Nothing was coming because I'd already decided. All I had to do was accept the decision. That's part of being a grown-up, you know. You have to make choices, permanent choices. And those choices sometimes put limitations on you. Choices are like time moving by, water passing under life's bridge. But for everything you let go of, life opens another door, something on the other side ready to be explored.

Mustin

Artie and the Jongleurs – 2004

One day a few months ago, I came home from work to find an envelope from a New York law firm buried in a handful of junk mail. The letter inside consisted of one paragraph:

> *As legal representative of the Jongleur family, Dartmouth, Nova Scotia, Canada, I believe you to be a direct descendant of Mr. Merle Jongleur, formerly of Nova Scotia. If I am correct in this, please contact me immediately at the number indicated above.*
>
> */s/ Justin Rathbone, Esq.*

"Why the frown?" Sandy asked me that night.

I pulled the letter from my shirt pocket and handed it to her. "It's a scam. Or maybe some trouble catching up to Merle."

"Better call," she said after reading it.

The next morning, I called from the jobsite and identified myself to the woman who answered. It took a while before Mr. Rathbone came on.

"Look," I began, irritable because of the wait, "Merle's long since gone, died back in eighty-eight. All he had was a run-down house and a worthless car, and they went to pay back taxes. The lawyer told me I'm not responsible for anything else." Rude, I know, but I had a half-dozen crew chiefs waiting.

Nonplussed, Rathbone replied, "This is regarding another subject altogether. Research for our client turned up your great-grandfather's death certificate. He was the older brother of Philippe Jongleur. Our firm is representing the Jongleur family in settlement of Philippe's estate. We need to resolve your part in the inheritance. To do so, I'll need proof of identity and lineage, sent to this address."

He wouldn't tell me more, but I promised to fax the necessary papers the next day. That night, I could feel Merle's presence as I went through those old papers—his body odor, the rancid breath—as palpable as in real life. I found my birth certificate and a yellowed copy of my mom Marie's. After putting them in an envelope with a photocopy of my driver's license, I managed to forget the whole affair and old Merle slipped back into his cave.

Three weeks later, the Rathbone guy left a message on our voice mail telling me an envelope with copies of the settlement would arrive soon. A courier delivered them the following evening, the details incredible.

The Jongleur heirs were to inherit three parcels of land, each having been in the family for generations, all three in Nova Scotia; one on Cape Breton, another in Dartmouth, the last near Amherst at the New Brunswick border. The Cape Breton parcel was relatively small, but wooded and highly desirable for vacation home development. The Amherst tract had once been prime farmland. The Dartmouth parcel was coastal, and included the family home, currently occupied by a Jacqueline d'Entremont. The last item was a lobster boat of Philippe's. The estate's value? Six million, Canadian, four and a half million in U.S. dollars, based on offers by development firms. My portion would be just over half a million, American, once pending sales were completed and taxes paid.

Oh, man. Even before I moved in with Sandy—and Mortie, the son Sandy and I had had when we were kids, back before I left for the Navy—I'd dreamed of striking out on my own, being my own boss. Land development, that was to be my future, without the stress and intrigue of a large corporate environment. But with little collateral, I had no chance of securing the necessary loans. With this? Now I could call my own shots.

Sandy was working late that night, handling a press conference for the governor on flood relief for back-to-back hurricanes that had blown inland and flooded North Carolina mountain communities, including Asheville. So I paced, reread the documents twice, paced some more. I'd never been able to get Merle's voice out of my head, and that night he kept whispering, Do it, sonny boy. Didn't I tell you to go to Nova Scotia?

I needed to talk to someone, anyone, to relieve me of the old man's chatter, so I called a number given in the settlement documents for this Jacqueline d'Entremont, Philippe's daughter. She answered, some tenseness in her tone after I identified myself, her inflections like Merle's, but more measured.

"I'm floored by this," I said. "Merle died destitute. I didn't think he had anything."

Her cryptic reply: "He should never have left."

"Well, he talked about returning," I went on. "He wanted my mom, Marie, to go with him. In fact, the day he died he asked me to go to Nova Scotia and tell the family."

"It would have been better if you had." Icicles hung on her words.

After hanging up, I realized the call hadn't been remotely welcome. If I'd gone there back in '88 as Merle had wanted and told them of his death, Philippe would've amended his will and Merle's share would've been divided among the other Jongleurs. Now they'll probably contest the will, I thought. Probate will cost me in legal fees. I'll end up without a dime, maybe in the hole. Old Merle's voice kept badgering, telling me to go, Sonny, go to Nova Scotia.

Sandy walked in tired from a sixteen-hour workday. She listened to my tale while we prepared for bed. You could tell her wheels were turning about this, but she wasn't nearly as excited as I was. So I kept on about it. "Don't you see? It's an opening. I can still get in on that

Elk Mountain development up in Asheville. I'll be able to call my own shots, be my own man."

"You are your own man," she said as she brushed her hair in front of the bathroom mirror.

"Not as far as your parents are concerned," I said. "They think I'm sponging. I'm your kept man, the mutt you rescued from across the tracks. As far as they're concerned, I may as well not even have a job."

That had always been my argument with her whenever we talked about a business venture of my own, but it was a ruse. If I were to tell her the real reason I needed more freedom—that my frequent bouts of insecurity, even irritation, occurred because I couldn't shake old Merle, that I needed lots of emotional elbow room when the voice came—she'd have known for sure I was an albatross. Nuts, surely.

She dropped the brush, took my hand. We moved to the bed's edge and sat. "Don't you understand yet, Artie? Nothing's going to come between us. Not your past, not my parents." She smiled, her fingers soft and warm against my face. "Not even that inheritance."

She was just trying to calm me down, I thought. "I can't believe you're not with me. I mean, who could possibly turn down—"

"I didn't say anything about turning it down. It's just that money doesn't solve anything. Look at Charlie."

Her brother had gone off the deep end after Harvard, had put a snowstorm of cocaine up his nose to keep a 24/7 edge in the commodities market. His parents had thrown money at his problems, paying through the nose for rehab after he'd lost his broker's license. Two weeks after his third rehab, he'd driven his Ferrari into a bridge column on Long Island, not enough of him left after the fire to reconstruct and send home for the funeral.

Okay, I thought, I have problems, but not Charlie's. Besides, mine weren't always a problem. "I've never had money to squander, the way Charlie did," I said. "I'm not irresponsible."

"I'm tired," she said. "Can we talk about this tomorrow?"

The next day, she took off in midafternoon to make scratch lasagna and salad for Mortie and me. I stumbled into the house from work after dark and was into my second beer and going on again about the will and my call to this Jacqueline woman. Then the phone rang.

"My name is Janine Guidry of Nova Scotia," the caller said. "You talked to my grandmother."

A picture flashed before me of the Jacqueline d'Entremont I'd previously talked to as a short shrew ranting redfaced about the uncouth American who was horning in on the family fortune. I eyed Sandy, deep into her salad making, then slipped from the kitchen.

"I suppose I'm persona non grata up there now," I said to Janine.

A laugh, sincerely good-natured, from the sound of it. She talked without accent, jammed her words together, the way a city dweller from the Northeast might. "Grandma's a wonderful woman, but a little curt sometimes. She's concerned that Nova Scotia's changing, and the remaining Jongleurs are having to adapt to stay afloat. It's been difficult for her, for the whole family."

I finished my beer and opened another, Sandy mouthing that dinner was ready. Janine continued, implying the family was open to some sort of deal regarding the will. I waved Sandy off about dinner. She and Mortie sat to eat, and I slid into my recliner in the den.

"So we were wondering," Janine said, "if you have time to come up. You are family, after all, and we'd like to meet you."

That left me not knowing what to say. She hoped we could connect the following week. The family, she said, was anxious to meet Merle's remaining descendant. This would be the first season the Jongleurs wouldn't be lobstering. Halifax would hold a festival, something called GrouTyme, and the younger Jongleurs felt like partying. I had no excuse really, and Merle kept whispering Uh huh, I told you, you can't get out of going to Nova Scotia now, so I accepted. Still, as I hung up, the idea of going there gave me an icy shiver.

Sandy's slate-blue eyes filled with amusement as I told her about the conversation.

"What do you suppose they want," I asked, "to wine and dine me, get me in a good enough mood to sign papers taking me out of the will?"

"Would you let them do that?"

"No," I said, "hell, no."

"Yeah," said Mortie, his adolescent voice cracking in mid-sentence, "kick some butt, Pop."

"Your father and I are talking," Sandy said, glaring.

Away from the table, Mortie would have dwarfed her, a tad under six feet after a summer growth spurt, ungainly but beginning to look and sound like a man. But he would still wither when she disciplined him. He swallowed hard and bent to his meal.

She turned her frown to me. "I guess you'll have to cancel another session."

I groaned, wishing she'd forget the two sessions with Dr. Dobbs I'd already missed this past month. Sandy and I were—are—in love, always have been. We've talked marriage ever since I moved in, but since Katie and I divorced, well, I've had resistance. Sandy had suggested a certain psychiatrist, to see if counseling would help. So I'd finally said, okay, I'll start the ball rolling. I'll see this Dr. Dobbs.

But once Lana Dobbs and I started talking, everything inside me seemed to fall apart. I wanted to quit my job. Even found it hard to hang in there with Sandy and Mortie. Just wanted to hole up somewhere. Disappear.

"It's emotional blockage," the good doctor told me. "We'll deal with it, so don't worry for the time being about changing your external situation."

We didn't seem to be getting anywhere, though; I was frustrated by her gestalt stuff, the isolating of every damned feeling, and why it was there.

Then a month ago, vertigo had set in. "It's rare," Lana told me, "but trauma from the past can manifest this way. Again, it's emotional."

At that point, something had to give. My supervisory position at Travelways didn't call for manual labor, but I was constantly off the ground on construction equipment, on partially built bridges, and the dizziness was dangerous for me. I knew Lana and I should press on with the sessions, but her chipping away at my unconscious was getting old. Which is why I'd been making excuses and missing sessions.

"Lana won't like my missing another one," I admitted.

"Neither will I," said Sandy.

"So you think I shouldn't go to Nova Scotia."

She patted her mouth with a napkin, sat back, and sighed. "You have to set your own priorities, Artie."

"Now you're evading. Tell me."

She looked away and sniffed—she usually did that to show disapproval. "I think you're too emotionally involved with this inheritance affair, that's all."

I said, no, it was the opening I'd been looking for, a chance to really make something of my life.

She turned to the soft voice she knew I'd listen to, the voice that always seemed to imply I was missing some important insight. "You realize, don't you, we don't need the money. You're trying to make a point about self-sufficiency that doesn't need to be made."

"You're living your dream," I replied, "so why can't I live mine?"

Then the teasing smile I've always been a sucker for. She pointed her fork at me and started singing an old Everly Brothers song I'd taught her, one Marie had taught me. "Dream, dream, dream, dream," she sang in her contralto.

Merle wasn't saying anything now, but the pressure of his presence was there all the same. "I'm going," I muttered. "They're family, for crying out loud, Merle's family, mine. The Jongleurs."

She pushed her plate away, sipped the last of her wine, poured more. "All right. You've never made peace with Merle, and I know you won't let it go. Maybe the trip will do you good."

"Go on, Pop," said Mortie. "Take the money, too. I'm gonna need a car pretty soon."

So I bought an airline ticket, arranged my work schedule, and that seemed to quiet Merle some.

The next Friday, I took off for Halifax. The trip was rough; we hit a storm, and my stomach flip-flopped with the sudden drops. Maybe flying had been the reason for my unease about the trip, I thought, maybe it had nothing to do with Merle's ghost sitting in the vacant seat beside me. I've never been comfortable with flying, but there I was on an airliner in the middle of hurricane season. Anyway, Dr. Dobbs had told me to confront such unease. "Give to it," she'd said. "One instance of it may hold the key to your blockage, but you may go through several episodes before you find release."

Luckily, I didn't have to make a scene on the plane. The pilot detoured, took us around then above the storm. Dusk had already pushed the sun to the western horizon when we arrived. A short, trim lady with long hair and dark skin like Marie's, maybe in her late twenties, held a sign with my name on it. An older and taller woman with similar features stood to one side, a girl of eight or so with her.

"I'm Janine," the younger woman said. She gave her sign to the girl and took my hand. Her smile seemed to imply tons good will. "John, my ex-husband," she said, "he wanted to be here too, more out of curiosity than anything else, I suppose, but he had a camping trip scheduled up north this weekend."

She introduced the other woman, her mother, Alice Boutier. We both turned to the girl, who was Janine's daughter.

"Hello," the girl said in her mini-voice, "my name's Mara," and she stuck out her hand as Janine had done.

I dropped to one knee, took the hand. "Hello," I said, "my name's Artie."

She was a miniature of her mother, the hair, the facial characteristics, the dark skin. My imagination had shifted into overdrive; I began to imagine her as Marie when she was a little girl. Then Mara abandoned all ceremony and threw her skinny arms around my neck.

She and I walked hand in hand, the women behind us talking in whispers, probably curious about this mysterious, missing Jongleur from the States, and amazed that Mara had taken to me so easily. I was wondering about the Nova Scotia Jongleurs, too, how they saw me. At baggage claim, a minor irony dawned. I began to chuckle. Janine cocked her head, and her smile slipped a bit.

"None of us are really Jongleurs," I said.

After a perplexed moment, she replied, "Not by name, I guess. But look at us, you have to know the blood's there."

Then for some reason, the need to impress them with our mutual connections struck home. "There's more than blood to it for me," I said. "Merle insisted on Jongleur as my middle name."

Alice nodded her approval. Janine's smile renewed. She led us to her Bronco, and drove us south toward Bedford Basin and Dartmouth.

They told me more about Philippe and the family as the miles passed. He'd lived to be ninety-seven, his wife Anna having died twenty years earlier. Philippe's mind had remained strong and, with Jacqueline's help, he'd managed the family's businesses. Alice and her husband Michel had been running the lobster boat. Janine and John had remained partners in an insurance claims business, the only ones for whom a livelihood now seemed a sure thing. So, with Philippe's passing, the family had decided to pool their resources and talents and start over.

"We've been a fishing family for generations," said Alice, seated in a ramrod pose beside me, glancing as I gripped the front seat at turns. "Before that, we farmed."

"But," said Janine, "even at our best, we were smalltime fishers. We couldn't compete with the big concerns. And we never modernized. We kept using the old-fashioned traps, the hand-over-hand retrieval."

"The Europeans hurt everybody," said Alice. "They fish as if there's no tomorrow."

"Tourism's the thing now," Janine said, "and we've decided to go with the flow."

Their plan? To use some of the money to renovate a pair of old houses in Dartmouth—Jacqueline's and the Boutiers'—turn them into bed and breakfasts. Janine would leave the insurance business to John and open a tourguide company, employing relatives and a few friends. I wondered aloud whether winters hurt tourism, but they told me winters were milder than Merle had led me to believe. And a raft of fall festivals brought in enough tourists to keep businesses afloat through the cold season. These festivals would be vital during the difficult first years of their new venture, and the family was considering establishing its own.

We stopped in front of the Boutiers' clapboard house. Inside, high ceilings and evening shadows gave the downstairs rooms the empty, somber feel of old Merle's house. After a fish and potatoes dinner, Michel and I sipped ales in front of the parlor fireplace. He's a pleasant, slightly overweight fellow who looks a lot like a younger Merle. We talked a long while about fishing, the storms that occasionally thrash Nova Scotia. Then, during a yarn about ghosts in the house, my sleeve went taut.

Mara eyed me. "Are you my uncle?"

I quickly plotted a path across the family tree and told her, "Cousins, we're cousins, Mara."

She ran to the kitchen, proclaiming her newfound knowledge to Janine. After a hushed conversation, she ran back, scrambled up, plopped into my lap, and kissed my cheek.

"Mama says we're kissing cousins," she explained.

That prompted a resonant laugh from Michel. "Just like her mama, that one. Not a shy bone in her."

She wriggled into a comfortable position, her head on my chest. A few minutes later, she fell asleep.

Maybe it was Mara's prompting, more likely the ale and food, but I began yawning, barely able to follow the remainder of Michel's ghost story. Janine took Mara, and Alice showed me to a bedroom, a cold space on the second floor. Outside its bay window lay a cove, moon reflections wriggling across the waters. The blankets she left were more than enough, and I slept until the sun had burned itself to a blinding white.

Downstairs, Alice informed me Jacqueline would arrive in a few minutes for a family meeting. "Coffee?" she asked. "We're waiting breakfast for them." I took the mug as Janine drove up with Jacqueline.

The old lady clasped my hand. Merle chuckled as she squeezed. She didn't speak, eying me as if I had just been caught cracking the family vault.

We ate with little talk. Alice brought out another pot of coffee and poured for each of us. Jacqueline's gaze bored into me, the others shifting as if sitting in a bed of nettles. She broke the silence without much of a wait.

"I won't mince words, Mr. Royal. Your inclusion in my father's will was an unpleasant surprise. We knew Merle's daughter had died, but we never anticipated you." She took a deep breath, sighed. "I believe Janine has told you something of our plans."

I nodded. She's all right, Sonny boy, Merle advised, his booming laugh echoing inside me. You'll see.

"Then you understand why your inclusion will work such a hardship on us."

Despite Merle's good humor, the old lady had me feeling defensive. So I decided to go on the offensive before she could press me further.

"I was invited to meet the family, ma'am," I said. "I thought this was going to be a friendly affair. But if you wanted to tell me to go to hell, you could've saved us both time and expense by putting it in a letter."

Shoes shuffled beneath the table, eyes flicking back and forth. Michel hid a smile behind one hand.

The old lady didn't turn red as I'd expected, and she didn't raise her voice. Instead, her shoulders slumped. She sighed. "The family will honor Father's will, if that's what you want."

Sandy would've told me my retort had been insecure overkill, and she'd've been right. "I'm sorry," I said, "I wish I knew what Merle would say if he were here. But the truth is, I was looking forward to the money. I have business plans of my own, and this was going to be a godsend."

"I did invite you, honestly, with no strings attached," said Janine. "But Grandmother's right, this will work a hardship on the family's future." She glanced to the old lady, then back. "I'm sorry if you feel violated." She began to stir her coffee dregs. "We've never been well off. I'd hoped to do more for Mara now. She doesn't have many things other children have."

"Deaths and inheritances are difficult," said Jacqueline, clearly trying to oil the waters she'd roiled. "I suppose there's no way to make them otherwise."

For a while, we avoided the subject. Michel rattled on about the lobster boat the family was to sell, how it was only eight years old, had been refurbished the previous year, how it handled the rough seas so well. Then he and Alice talked between themselves about whether their house would suffice as a bed and breakfast without the planned renovation. Janine and Jacqueline made small talk. Mara listened, and her brown eyes kept returning to me. I was enjoying her pretending to be grown-up.

Over more toast, jam, and coffee, an idea slowly occurred.

"Look," I said, "there may be a way out of this. Merle wouldn't have wanted any of you to suffer because of Philippe's being so evenhanded with the estate. I'm thinking you should incorporate, assign each heir a percentage of ownership."

Silence. But I did note Jacqueline softening further. "Ma'am," I said to her, "I know you've been calling the shots for the family, but you could let things be more cooperative now. You could draw up an agreement, allow each heir a part of the family's overall profits each year. If necessary, they could plow those back into the company. If you could do that, I might be willing to leave my part of the inheritance as a percentage of ownership, too."

With a year or two of good luck and industry, I calculated, my part of the profits might amount to a steady twenty or thirty grand a year. That would provide collateral for a loan to finance my development dream.

Janine started to speak. Jacqueline waved her to silence. "You do seem to have a good business sense, Mr. Royal. A very creative suggestion. Let us talk among ourselves."

Everyone seemed to spring from the table at once. They trooped into the parlor and closed the door. Thirty minutes later, they emerged, all smiles. Jacqueline appeared last, gave me a faint nod and said, "I'll take the night to make a decision."

Janine took my arm. "You've got to see the city. Come on."

So I climbed into the back of the Bronco with Mara. We took Jacqueline home, a large but unassuming two-story on a clean, well-kept waterfront street. Then Janine drove us to the harbor and we took the ferry to Halifax.

I was surprised at how comforting it was to smell the sea up close again, to hear the waves slapping against the hull, to feel the pitching and rolling, and I hardly noticed my vertigo and white-knuckled grip on the railing. We dallied in the old town, visited an ancient Anglican church and an urban park, then a museum. After that, we wandered the streets, drank coffee, had lunch in a quiet, sunlit café. The harbor before us swarmed with boats. Incoming breezes pushed the strong, organic sea smell down each street as we continued to walk. I had to think of Brest, of Naples, even of the Middle Eastern ports I'd visited while in the Navy. The ships, the buoys, the terns and gulls, they stirred me in a way I hadn't felt for a long time.

Mara chattered, pointing out sights she was sure I'd like, fumbling over the names with a little girl's affected confidence. Janine walked ahead. As the sky dimmed, we ducked into a pub, Mara riding my shoulders.

Michel waved from a booth. The pub had the damp, dark ambience of such places around the world, and its woody smell mingled with that of ale and fried foods. After a few minutes of family chat, Michel asked, "You want to go with us to the GrouTyme, don't you?"

"Oh, yeah," I said, "the festival."

"Alderney Landing. Lots of music. You step dance?"

The Jongleur in my blood rose at the mention, and I quietly tapped out some of the Chéticamp beneath the table. Merle's fiddling seemed to echo about us; I could even sense rosin particles riding those imagined strings of his.

"I remember a little of it," I said. "Mom taught me. Merle used to play the fiddle, and she'd dance me around the living room."

"Okay then," said Michel, "we're going to have us some fun, Acadian style."

"We need to eat first," said Janine. Let's order."

I had something like a shrimp étoufée, and it was delicious, the shrimp fresh and clean and firm. Janine had a salmon sandwich, Michel a platter of fried sole and chips, and Mara picked from their plates. By the time we were through, darkness had fallen. All that was left of the harbor was a slur of bells and foghorns.

We took the ferry back to Dartmouth and met Alice on a corner a block away from Alderney Landing. Already, you could smell the confections and hear the music, the clatter of feet. We worked our way through the crowd, following the music as if we were the children of Hamelin. Michel stopped us at a large stage. The band had ceased playing to confer, and now bounded into another tune, one I recognized from Merle's fiddling. The ensemble left little of the tune's complex interplay between rhythm and melody to the imagination. Alice and Michel joined the dancers. Both were sure-footed, Alice prim above the waist, Michel giving his whole body to the music.

"Are you sure you can dance these?" Janine asked above the blare, one foot already into the beat.

"Come on," I said.

We joined the others, Mara's shoes clacking along with us at the crowd's periphery. I lost the step at first, but as my feet moved, they remembered. When it ended, we fell into each other, laughing and hugging.

"Now me," Mara yelled.

The fiddler kicked off another tune. I took Mara's tiny hands, and off we went, she as nimble as her mother. Again the dance swept us away, nothing in our world but music. See? Merle admonished, you can dance yourself happy, huh?

"You're pretty good," Janine said afterward. "You must've done this a lot when you were younger."

"Merle," I gasped, chest heaving, "he wouldn't let me alone. Just had to fiddle. He fiddled, I danced." This night, I'd danced as if on air, and it had left me giddily happy, a feeling I hadn't had in a long time.

While the next band set up, we walked to the quay for a bit of fresh air. The bay breeze had turned chilly, so we returned. An older man made announcements on stage, then told a joke that didn't go over well. The new bandmembers introduced themselves, and a moment later they tore into an up-tempo tune. Their music was different, more edgy, modern, yet the rhythms were recognizable. Across the sea of dancers, we watched Alice and Michel step cautiously into the dance, make a turn, then stop. Michel waved in frustration at the band, and he and Alice retreated.

"Well, I like their music," said Janine.

"Me too," said Mara.

I took both their hands and dragged them in. Janine looked at me in an odd way, then shrugged and began to dance. Mara giggled. This was something new, a dance you wouldn't call authentic, reminding me of Merle's drunken fiddle improvisations. But those around us howled encouragement as the music's tempo increased. When the tune ended, Janine, Mara and I gasped as we clung to one another. A hand gripped my shoulder.

"That was something," said Michel. "Where'd you learn that?"

"I guess we just fell into it," said Janine, "don't you think so, Artie?"

"The feet," I said, still trying to catch my breath, "the feet did it."

They laughed, even Alice. Mara gave a squeal and jumped into my arms, legs around me, tried to kiss me on the mouth. She missed, caught my chin.

The set ended and we gathered, Michel yawning for effect. "It's late," he said. "Gotta get on home." We made our way back to the streets, the band's playing dimmed, the harbor's own music rising. As I climbed out at Alice and Michel's, Janine reminded me: "Grandma will be over for breakfast again."

I woke early, a prism of sun on my face from the harbor-facing window. Downstairs, Alice and Michel busied themselves with breakfast. Janine and Jacqueline arrived moments later, and we ate in strained formality. With the eggs and toast and ham gone, we stirred our coffee in silence, waiting.

Jacqueline cleared her throat. "I've considered your proposal, Mr. Royal. As I said yesterday, it was thoughtful and creative." She sipped.

My stomach began to sink. Something in her tone told me she was going to refuse my suggestion, or counter with something unappealing. Sandy was right; I shouldn't have come. All I'd accomplished was setting myself up for another disappointment. No, Merle whispered, hold that tongue, boy, hear what she has to say.

"My problem," Jacqueline continued, "was my own idea of how best to use Father's estate for our family's future. I had long since made up my mind, I'm afraid, and your inclusion, even your suggestion, complicated things."

Prior to this moment, I'd had no idea how Alice, Michel and Janine really felt about my sudden appearance in their lives. But as Jacqueline spoke, I noted subtle body movements, barely suppressed facial expressions. Without question, Alice would be against me, Janine for. Michel seemed unreadable in that regard, but the situation clearly amused him. Their inclinations hardly mattered, though; Jacqueline would tell us her decision at the end of this preamble, and we'd find our separate ways of accepting it.

"I won't contest the will," Jacqueline said, with emphasis on won't. "And I will take Mr. Royal's suggestion, at least to a point." She turned to me. "I suppose you're expecting some immediate yearly return to use in your own business venture."

"Yes," I replied.

"I'm afraid I cannot agree to that."

All eyes were on me, Merle growling, Hush, boy, listen.

"There's a strong likelihood of a decent living for us," Jacqueline explained, "but with advertising and startup costs, there's very little chance for profit, at least immediately. Tourism is a competitive business here."

The sinking feeling returned, but irritation began its boil, too—she was going to use my idea and leave me out of the business. The others fumbled with their mugs, shuffled feet, and twisted in their chairs.

"But you've shown me your motives are in the best interests of us all, and for that I'm grateful. Because your heart is in the right place, I propose something more symbolic than substantial in return. Unless Michel has strong objections, I want you to have the boat."

"Huh," said Michel, surprise stripping him of his amusement.

Alice said nothing, showed nothing, except a clamped-shut jaw.

Janine eyed Jacqueline then Michel, then me. She seemed delighted, but she'd always seemed affable. The broader than usual smile may have been her way of showing surprise.

My initial annoyance led to a fog of questions. The old woman's taking my idea and offering a lobster boat in return? Owning your own vessel, operating it on the ocean, as any ex-sailor would have to admit, had a certain appeal. But I lived inland now, worked building roads. What would I do with it? And did Jacqueline intend this to take the place of Merle's inheritance? Something about the odd offer warned of danger.

"Well, sure," Michel said, stumbling over his words, "ah, it's okay, I guess. Sure."

Jacqueline's gaze once again fixed me.

I wanted to put her off, think this through. A cold chill knifed through me, turned to dread. And time was crowding me; I had to return home the following day. Despite my unease, I said, "I don't know fishing boats. Maybe seeing it would help."

"I'd planned to drydock it this week," said Michel, "but it's still at the pier. We can take it out this afternoon."

"Can I go?" Mara asked.

Somehow, I couldn't imagine her not going. "If your mother says it's all right," I said.

"I have to drive to Breton Park, pick up John," said Janine. "Won't be back until late. Guess it'll be okay."

As we began pushing chairs back, Jacqueline raised a hand. "We will incorporate as you suggested, Mr. Royal. And please, whether you take the boat or not, you'll be a partner in our venture. If and when we begin to show profits, I'll make sure you receive a proportional share. Our lawyer will send you annual reports."

Janine hugged me, and then Michel gripped my hand. Alice ventured a friendly smile. Jacqueline circled the table, beaming for the first time, her hands warm on my forearms. "Welcome to our family. It's too bad you don't live nearby."

Minutes later, we lurched away in Michel's pickup, Mara on my lap, headed for the docks. There, my idea of fishing boats took a hit. The boat seemed tiny, smaller than its thirty-five foot length. The hull had been covered in fiberglass, maybe a year before, and painted an aqua blue. A white wheelhouse rose just forward of amidships, a cramped looking structure, making the boat seem even smaller. The aft deck was nondescript, level for hauling lobster traps, lines and buoys, with nothing to restrain workers.

"It's over twelve foot in the beam, four foot of draft, empty," Michel said. "Sleeps four, got a sounder and a CB. The inside's finished in oak." He nodded proudly.

We stepped aboard. Michel started the engine, cast off, and backed out. We made our way down the Eastern Passage to the Atlantic. For a while, I stayed with him in the wheelhouse, Mara on my hip so she could see incoming smacks on the horizon, the lines of buoy, the gulls. As Michel steered to the open sea, my concern over the boat's size disappeared. I was eager for the smell of diesel and salt air again, so I took Mara forward. Choppy water slapped the hull, the deck wet and slick. Edging up, Mara's hand in mine, we reached the bow. I gripped the railing, Mara now clinging to my leg.

Our proximity to the water made the sea's effect stronger. It was as I'd remembered it, only better, more intimate, as if I were being drawn closer to an old friend. Salt spray stung us. I licked it off my lips. Mara giggled at my clumsiness, then she began using one of my swaying legs as if it were a gymnastic apparatus. The boat throbbed, its two hundred horsepower engine propelling us forcefully along.

This was it. This was what I'd been missing since I was a kid, the thing busyness on Navy ships had managed to deny me. I thought of my old bike, racing down South Main, the wind in my face and ears, the detached, free feeling.

Then Mara howled. She had let go of me and had leaned over the railing. The boat had reared atop a wave, clapped the water as it fell. She'd lost her balance, flipped over the top rail. I lunged, grabbed one hand.

The combination of my lunging and the boat's tossing brought nausea. My grip weakened. Goddamn you, Merle. You want me to die, and this child too?

"Marie!" I yelled, realizing my error as I said it. "Mara, lift your feet! Reach with them, catch the bottom rail!"

She thrashed, accomplished the feat. But, woven between the rails, she couldn't drop to the deck.

The boat lurched. Michel had cut the power to a crawl, the bow nosing into a wave. The movement threw Mara backward and onto the deck. My vision skipped like a movie from a reel of old, brittle film. I could barely make out her hands on the gunwale. Then I heard her feet dancing as she scrambled backwards and into Michel's arms.

The boat surged upward on another wave. The top rail bent me double. I felt the sickness of falling. The cold North Atlantic water jolted me—minutes of this could prove fatal. Still, instinct had me push away from the boat so I wouldn't be hit by it or caught in the propeller wash.

This was Merle's legacy to me, I thought as I rose on the next wave. Everything about him had led me to this. I'd always staggered under the weight of his personality, then I'd drowned in his illness, and that immersion would now become fatal.

The next wave swallowed me. I went under. See? said Merle. Things making sense now? I kicked my way to the surface, spewed water, began to thrash. You got to dance, boy, said Merle. Why you think I taught you all them dances? I began to laugh as I flailed, maybe because of the cold thrilling its way through me, or maybe it was the ludicrous thought of dancing in the water. Old fool. I'm taking a bath, Merle, going to get your stink off me for good. The icy water had me more deranged than normal, I guess. You avoiding things, Sonny, Merle replied. This about you, not me.

Michel's life preserver hit the water inches away, skipped into my face. Blood trickled from my nose and onto my tongue, and I couldn't tell the difference between the tastes of that and seawater. Then my derangement gave to panic. I had to seize the ring, now, before shock set in.

Then, for a moment, the ocean calmed, its swells settling into gentle undulations. In this moment, I seemed nothing more than a drop, a minuscule portion of this icy expanse. I had no reason to fear anything about it, as if fifty pairs of hands surrounded me, buoying me, allowing me to fill with the sea's energy.

You got it now? Merle asked. You ready to fill that big hole in you? You part of something bigger than yourself now? All right, guess I can go.

I bobbed upward, as if some weight had dropped from me. I caught a glimpse of a shadow, moving at the edge of my vision, something I'd associated with Merle since the day he'd died.

Michel tossed the ring again. "Grab hold!" he yelled.

The sea's bracing effect had left me. I gasped for air, took in water. But somehow I managed to slither into the ring, felt the line jerk taut, then the intermittent tugs as Michel dragged me to him. His hands gripped mine, and he pulled me aboard. We sat panting in a puddle of water.

"Mara!" Michel yelled, "go below and get a blanket." He dragged me into the wheelhouse, took the blanket, and wrapped me. I began to shake. He handed me a cup of whiskey. That helped, a little. Minutes later, the shaking returned. I couldn't control it. "Come on," he said, "let's get you below. Got a heater there."

It took a half hour for the convulsions to end. Michel handed me a cup of whiskey-laced coffee and, after bolting it, I began to think about what had happened.

Each second in the water resonated as clearly as the ring of crystal. Merle had been right: this had been about me—some inner void I'd alternately ignored and protected over the years. I suppose the immensity of it had reminded me of an ocean, and that subconscious imagining had led me to become a sailor. But until now, I couldn't have risen above it the way an adult perspective demands, understood it as the losses I'd suffered as a boy. So it had had to lure me again, to Nova Scotia.

This thinking, I finally decided, this elevated rationale, was also some mental reaction to the cold, itself a temporary form of insanity. Odd, but the water *had* seemed aware. Alive, as if it had consciously christened me, then buoyed me, so Michel could save me. Maybe in some primitive manner, in the way poets understand things, the sea *is* alive. All I knew for certain was I had to remain at its disposal, at least for a while longer.

We docked in late afternoon. Michel had called Alice over the boat's CB, had her bring food and a change of clothes for me. With all of us back at the Boutiers', Alice scurried about, preparing an aromatic stew, Mara at her knees and ankles. From across the kitchen table, Michel instructed me in navigation's intricacies, in the boat's behavior in currents, tides, winds. Beyond the few motes registering from his instruction, another idea came to me, something I hoped would cement my relationship with these newfound relations.

A few minutes later, Janine drove up with Jacqueline.

"Mama, Mama," Mara called out, "I almost fell in the water!"

Janine picked her up.

"Artie saved me, Mama," Mara said.

"It's my fault," I said at the end of Mara's telling. "I'm so sorry. I'd have died if anything had happened to Mara."

Janine offered a cautious smile, then Alice called us to the table. Her stew, along with homemade bread and a couple of ales took what was left of the chill from me. The trauma of my nearly drowning began to fade. After dinner, Michel and I had more ale, and Mara again jabbered away, retelling her tale to anyone who would listen. Finally, all eyes turned to me, Jacqueline as wary as a deer in a glade.

"Mrs. d'Entremont," I said, "I think I'll take the boat. But I have one stipulation—actually two. I'll take it only as a trade. And I'll need Michel to help me sail it home."

Murmurs rose. Jacqueline waved them away, smiled, ever so faintly. "We have Mi'kmaq blood, Mr. Royal. They're the ones the Acadians first met here, you know. Trades are always welcome. What do you have in mind?"

Michel chuckled. "Yeah, I want to know, what do you think is worth a boat?"

"Let me make a phone call." I returned to my room, found my cell phone.

Sandy laughed. "A lobster boat? You can't be serious."

I told her my proposed trade. "You don't think Mortie will have a problem, do you?"

"Hardly. It's still in great shape. Anyway, all he talks about these days is getting a car. Are you thinking of selling the boat?"

"No, it's important for me to have it. Maybe later for Mortie, too."

"All right," she said, sighing, clearly not understanding. "I'll put Mortie on a plane tomorrow. You realize this is going to cost, don't you? Boat berths in Wilmington aren't cheap."

"Well, it's important," I repeated.

"How long are you going to keep Mortie out of school?"

"Let's say all week."

I guess at that point I must've sounded more excited than normal, because she laughed. "What's happened, Artie? You sound different."

"Tell you when we get home."

At the table, the hum of voices fell silent. "Come on, man," said Michel, "tell us what the trade is."

"It's arriving tomorrow afternoon. With my son."

Michel wanted to be there, and Janine was equally overcome with curiosity. I'd insisted she keep Mara out of school. Mortie stepped off the plane, passed through customs, unusually effervescent, even for the extrovert he is. He insisted for the first time that his name was Mort, as Sandy's father's had been. I introduced him, and we all turned toward the baggage carousel.

It took a half hour before a man rolled the bicycle through to us.

I took Mara's hand and knelt. "Honey, it's a family heirloom. It used to be my mother's, then mine, then Mort's. Now it's yours."

Her mouth fell open. She reached out, touched it. Then she seized it with both hands, squealing her excitement.

"I'll be," said Janine.

"Now that's a fine trade," said Michel.

It took three days to finalize the paperwork, a complicated affair, since the boat was moving to the States. The following morning Mort, Michel, and I brought our bags on board, along with enough water and food for a weeklong voyage, although Michel said we would probably arrive in Wilmington in three, possibly four days. "No storms coming, so we might decide to take longer," he said with a wink.

The boat's new name, *Merle's Marie*, had been painted on the stern the previous day. I would keep it up, take it out until Mort was old enough to assume ownership.

He'd suffered, too, during my twelve years away from Sandy and him, and somehow I felt his being on the boat on the open sea might help heal that. Maybe make his maturing a little easier than mine had been.

We said our goodbyes and cast off. The boat pitched as Michel guided us to the open sea. Mort began to sway with its movement like a seasoned sailor.

Michel glanced to him. "You want to take the wheel, young fella?"

Mort looked to me, acknowledged my shrug with a grin.

"Just hold it steady right now," said Michel. "When we're out a ways, I'll show you how to come to new headings. You know anything about navigating?"

Mort was full of questions. Michel guided Mort's attention to the wheel and compass as the sea tugged us this way and that. The diesel engine's rumble remained even and strong. I slipped out and went forward.

Nothing had changed for me on this trip, I realized, despite my flirtation with death, the glimpse of some inner darkness, except that I had shed old Merle's ghost. And I realized the Jongleurs would probably never show enough profit to make my development scheme real. It would remain that, a figment, something I'd hold onto to help me bide my life's day-to-day tedium.

But Nova Scotia and the Jongleurs had drawn me in, especially Mara and Janine. I knew somehow I'd be returning. But the family feel I'd experienced, would it really be the same when I did? For me, family's always been such a slippery mix of hope and disappointment.

And nothing in this Nova Scotia adventure could help bridge the gulf I'd created between Sandy and me so many years ago when I'd left her for the Navy. Mort's bursting at the seams now, for newness, for adventure, the way I've always been, the way I'll always be. That'll no doubt add to the problems between Sandy and me.

Oh, well. Maybe if Sandy and I had never shared that year of teen abandon, or maybe if we'd stayed together after high school, gone to college together, I'd be a different, simpler person. Maybe I'd be able to compromise, to accept, to give to her, the way she's done to raise Mort. My burden now that Merle's gone is the fear that I'm never going to find the firm footing ordinary life seems for everyone else, no matter how hard I try.

A stiff wind raced up my back from the following sea, and I went below for a jacket. Returning, I almost ran to the bow, eager to take in more of this fertile sea air. Above, the sky had dropped a dome of deep autumn blue about us, a thin white streak its only blemish, the sun soft on my face and hands. The land flattened and fell away. Then the last birds shrunk to dots off the starboard bow. Nothing lay ahead but two shades of blue, one above, one below.

Talk about great. It was the perfect day for sailing.

Discussion Guide

• In the1980 section, how does Artie's mother, Marie, figure into his life?

• How is Merle's music like Artie's Blue bike?

• In high school, is Artie wise to be involved with Sandy? How about in the 2004 section?

• In the 2002 section, Artie has his first wife, Katie, learn a bit of verse by John Donne. How do you think this applies to Artie's Life? To Katie's?

• Why do you think Artie took the boat in the 2004 section? What did it mean to him?

• Following Merle's death, why couldn't Artie get Merle's voice out of his head?

• How is the tone of each of the book's four sections different?

• What was Artie's attraction to the sea?

ABOUT THE AUTHOR

Bob Mustin has had a brief naval career and a longer one as a civil engineer and has been a North Carolina Writers Network writer-in-residence at Peace College under the late Doris Betts' guiding hand. In the early 90s he was the editor of a small literary journal, The Rural Sophisticate, based in Georgia. His work has appeared extensively in print and electronic publications

To learn more about Bob Mustin, visit:
Website: www.bobmustin.com
Blog: bobmust.wordpress.com